LITTLE WOMEN IN INDIA

by Jane Nardin

"BOOKS ARE MADE OUT OF OTHER BOOKS."

LITTLE WOMEN IN INDIA

First published in 2012 by
New Dawn Publishers Ltd
292 Rochfords Gardens
Slough, Berkshire SL2 5XW

www.newdawnpublishersltd.co.uk

newdawnpublishersltd@gmail.com

ISBN 9781-908462-07-7

CHAPTER ONE: THE SISTERS

It was Christmas Eve in the year 1856, and the four May sisters were sitting together on the comfortable veranda of their bungalow in Shivapur. Purple passion flowers and bougainvillea with its bright fuschia blossoms twined about the carved posts of the veranda, while delicate maidenhair ferns in pots screened the girls from the view of passers by. In northern India, November through March is the season of cool weather, so the temperature was pleasant.

By the 1850s, the British East India Company had established its rule over most of India. Its employees called it "*the* Company," as if it were the only company in the world that counted for anything. Every one of the Company's "stations" governed a territory inhabited by many thousands of Indians. Yet no Indian held a position of power in the Company. *All* the important officials at the Shivapur station, including the May girls' father, were English.

Shivapur's English families lived in the "civil lines," where the wide streets were laid out in a rigid grid pattern. Through the fresh, green branches of the neem trees that fringed the Mays' lawn, several stately bungalows could be glimpsed. The crowded, disorderly native district, with its twisting alleyways, was not visible. Nor was the cantonment, where a regiment of native soldiers and their English officers lived in barracks.

"I don't see the point of having Christmas if we can't have presents," grumbled Catherine, looking up from the novel she was reading.

"And how annoying it is that we're too poor to send to Paris for the latest fashions," lamented Jane, patting her gold-streaked curls.

"Well, I don't think it's fair that other girls can buy all the paints they want, when I draw so much better than they do," Elizabeth said angrily.

"But at least we are all at home, where we can help poor Mama deal with her difficulties," said little Fanny in a self-denying tone.

"Yes, it's wonderful that Catherine has *finally* come back from London. But it's not true that we are *all* at home," Jane argued. "Papa won't be with us again for many months, not until the end of the hot weather."

"And with all this unrest, he really is in a bit of danger, out there in the countryside settling disputes. If there was trouble with the natives, how could he protect himself?" Elizabeth wondered.

"I don't know," Fanny said, sounding worried. "But I *do* know that Papa doesn't want us to give presents this Christmas because we simply *must* start paying his debts." She was darning one of her mother's stockings as she spoke.

"I know Papa is in debt, but I don't really know how bad it is. You never mentioned it in the letters you sent me in London. Tell me everything," Catherine said encouragingly. She was fond of her anxious, conscientious little sister.

Fanny was eager to excuse their father. She said that when dear Papa came out to India to work for the Company, he was really just a boy. So his small salary seemed like a fortune to him. When people told him that he would lose face if he didn't keep at least five servants, he decided to hire seven. They also said he had to have a palanquin with a bunch of bearers to carry him around in it. So he got one. And he naturally couldn't resist buying thoroughbred horses.

"I suppose," Elizabeth said, "that Papa didn't even notice he was spending more than he earned. All he ever thinks about, even now, is getting through his paperwork."

"I'm afraid so," Fanny agreed, "and the next thing he knew, he was borrowing money at a horrible rate of interest. Then there was his marriage to Mama, who didn't have a penny. Then it was the huge expense of sending Catherine to school in England for eight whole years, and then —"

"But Papa *didn't* send you girls abroad—and he's brought me home now so that I can teach you and save the cost of a governess," Catherine interrupted in a startled tone. "I am going to start as soon as the holidays are over."

"Yes, that is an economy," Fanny said, "but it isn't enough. We must save every rupee we can. Poor Papa feels so guilty for having lived beyond his means all these years. He is determined to do the right thing now. We must help him by being as selfless as possible."

"I hate the idea of selflessness," snapped Elizabeth. "I'm not like you, Fanny, always congratulating myself on putting others first. Why shouldn't *I* come first, I'd like to know?"

"Mama has had to make sacrifices, too," Jane said, "and I'm not sure she enjoyed it any more than Lizzie would. It must have been very shaming to be sent out to India at seventeen, on the fishing fleet."

Catherine looked mystified as she asked her sister what the "fishing fleet" might be. Her ladylike mother had certainly never worked as a fisherwoman, if such a word even existed! Did it? Catherine liked inventing new words.

"Oh, Catherine, how little you know about India! You've spent so much time in London. It's almost as if you'd never lived here at all!" Jane exclaimed. "The 'fishing fleet' is what they call the ships that bring girls from England to 'fish' for husbands."

"Yes," said Elizabeth, "and by the time Mama arrived, Papa was quite a catch."

"Why was that?" Catherine asked.

"Because he had become a three-hundred-pounder."

"Surely not," Catherine objected. "Papa *is* a bit tubby, but he certainly doesn't weigh three hundred pounds. And he must have been *much* thinner when he and Mama got married."

Elizabeth said that the name had nothing to do with size. "Three-hundred-pounder" was a slang term for any Company official whose wife was entitled to a three hundred pound pension if he died. Translated into rupees, three hundred pounds a year was a lot of money.

"Imagine marrying for such a reason," Jane said, glancing up briefly over the delicate lace she was crocheting. "I shall certainly marry for love. Perhaps I'll be lucky enough to fall in love with someone rich."

"It would be painful," said Fanny seriously, "to feel that one could relieve one's family of a burden by making a loveless marriage. Still, it can hardly be right to marry without love."

"Mama did it, in any case," said Elizabeth emphatically, "and now we learn that instead of a husband who was kind enough to die and leave her well off, she has one who is hopelessly in debt."

Jane cheered up. "Well, we each have a pound, so perhaps Papa wouldn't mind if we bought presents for ourselves, provided we don't expect anything from Mama. I shall get one of the new *solar topees* trimmed with pelican skin and feathers. Papa *did* say that ladies who wear them have a demented air, but he knows nothing about fashion."

"I shall buy *The Warden*, the new novel that's causing a flurry in England. It may give me some ideas for my own writing," Catherine said, waving her pen and splashing her skirt with ink.

"For me, a small tube of carmine. It's a very expensive color," Elizabeth added, as she put the finishing touches to a sketch of an imaginary English landscape. "I think that I shall give my pound to dear Papa," said Fanny, but her sisters showed no sign of wishing to follow her example.

The girls rose from their long cane chairs to welcome their mother, as she returned from paying a round of calls. Mrs. May, a plump lady of forty, wore an afternoon dress of pearl gray *barège*. Her spreading skirts were supported by steel-hooped petticoats.

Mrs. May smiled at her daughters with love and anxiety. How would she manage to find husbands for them all, she wondered.

Jane, at sixteen, would not pose a problem. With her graceful figure and big blue eyes, her pink and white complexion and her sun-kissed hair, she was a truly beautiful girl. She was already beginning to attract attention from the young army officers and officials who lived at the station. And she clearly enjoyed masculine society.

But seventeen-year-old Catherine might well prove troublesome. Though her hawklike, intelligent face was handsome enough, her angular figure spoiled its effect. Would *anyone* care to court such an unnaturally tall young lady? And to make matters worse, Catherine didn't care a bit about her appearance. It wouldn't do to have one's daughter get a reputation as a flirt, but a girl could show some interest in men without disgracing herself.

Elizabeth's pretty face was set off by thick, wavy black hair, and her dark eyes sparkled with vitality. But even at fifteen, she had a disturbingly fierce temper. A prudent man might well hesitate before making an offer of marriage to such a spitfire. And it was upsetting that Elizabeth spent so much time hunched over a table, painting and drawing. She might become near sighted or even round shouldered. But no one could make Elizabeth do anything she didn't want to do!

Fanny was thirteen and, unfortunately, rather plain. Her smooth, straight hair was the same pale color as her eyes. Her lips were pale too. She was small for her age, and her figure was completely undeveloped. But thank heavens, she would do as she was told when the time came.

Mrs. May sighed as she walked from veranda to parlor, followed by her daughters.

The parlor was cool and gloomy. The bungalow's thick mud brick walls and small windows kept out the heat during the hot weather, when outdoor temperatures skyrocketed to unbelievable heights. Unfortunately, they also kept out the light. Inside the parlor, the rough beams supporting the bungalow's thatched roof were visible. Plaster ceilings had been vetoed, because the spaces above them provided a home for mice and rats, which were much feared by Mrs. May. It was not pleasant to hear those little feet pattering about overhead.

Mrs. May lighted the oil lamps, giving the room a more homelike air. She walked toward the divan, carefully avoiding an unsteady little table with legs made out of antelope horns.

"Well, girls, how have you been today? I meant to come back earlier, but my calls took longer than I expected. I thought that I'd just leave my visiting card. But Mrs. Brown *and* Mrs. Barnfather wanted to show off their Christmas preparations, so I was forced to pay two real visits. I was *so* humiliated when I had to admit that we aren't giving gifts to mark the day because we need to economize. Mrs. Brown even accused me of insulting our Savior. She is always hinting that we are not as pious as we should be."

"Perhaps we can turn the tables on *her* in church tomorrow, by singing the hymns in particularly loud voices and casting our eyes up to heaven," Elizabeth suggested.

"Lizzie, you can't use divine service as an opportunity to carry on a petty personal feud," Fanny said instantly.

"Oh, can't I? It might at least keep me awake. Reverend Brown's sermons are incredibly boring."

"Yes," Catherine agreed, "they really are awful. I couldn't believe it when he preached on the text, 'My brother Esau is a hairy man, but I am a smooth man.' How could anyone find spiritual comfort in *that* remark? Even if it *does* come from the Bible!"

"Girls, girls," Mrs. May put in hastily, "please don't be irreverent. Suppose someone were to hear you! I've got a treat for you after supper. The *chuprassi* who delivers messages for Papa brought us a letter from him today." She patted her little reticule to indicate the letter's location.

The girls smiled brightly, for despite his eccentricities, they loved their father. And Mrs. May had grown fond of the man she had married for the sake of security alone.

Inder, the butler—or *khansama* he was called in Hindi—summoned the family to a dinner of peppery mulligatawny soup, broiled fish, roast chicken with bread stuffing, lamb curry with rice, mutton pie with vegetables, rice pudding, and savory cheese, washed down with red wine. Food was much cheaper in India than in England, and this sort of eating was the usual thing among the British. Fanny often thought they might eat less and give more to the poor. She saw so many starving Indian children, so many beggars. But she said nothing, not wishing to appear critical of her own countrymen.

After dinner, Mrs. May read her husband's letter aloud.

"My dear wife and daughters,

I have exciting news for you. Last night, a group of *dacoits* (or bandits!) slipped into our tent to steal my valuables. My servant gave the alarm, but when we seized the *dacoits*, we found that they had oiled their bodies! They literally slipped through our fingers and escaped with the loot. It is sad to have lost so much property at a time when we must practice economy at home.

I hoped that the local peasants would betray the *dacoits*, but so far this has not happened. Perhaps the peasants are not as loyal to me as I thought they were? No, that cannot be true. The native instinctively reveres honorable English gentlemen like myself. So I am sure they would tell me the thieves' identity if they knew it.

Dearest family, though I cannot return to you for many months, my thoughts are with you. It seems a long time to wait, but we may all do our duty, so that these hard days will not be wasted.

Catherine and Elizabeth must suppress their ambitions and remember that no female has ever become a first-rate writer or painter. A woman may tell bedtime stories to her children or decorate her parlor with her sketches, but she should never come before the public as a professional artist. That would be disgracefully immodest! Jane must combat her vanity and her longing for luxuries. And even good little Fanny must work harder at the pianoforte, so that someday she can play soothing airs to her husband.

I know you girls will be loving children to your mother, do your duty faithfully, and conquer your selfish tendencies so beautifully, that when I come home I will be fonder than ever of my little women."

Fanny sniffled when they came to that part, but her sisters did not. Elizabeth was opening her mouth to say that she had no intention of conquering her selfish tendencies, when Mrs. May continued reading:

"You will be happy to hear that I have not accumulated any arrears of paperwork since I left home, though superhuman exertions have been necessary to produce this satisfactory state of affairs.

Your loving father,

Theophilus May, Examining Magistrate of Shivapore."

"My heavens," Mrs. May said briskly, "I wish your Papa had paid less attention to his paperwork and more to his debts. When I told Mrs. Brown about his money troubles, her face glowed like a Chinese lantern with delight. And that was *quite* unbecoming, for her nose is red and shiny at the best of times."

"Indeed it is, and Susan Brown has inherited it. Susan looks as if her clothes had been stuck on her back with a pitchfork," said Jane with some satisfaction.

Catherine laughed. "Papa is right about your vanity, Jane, but he is utterly wrong about women writers. Look at Currer, Ellis, and Acton Bell. No one in England had the faintest idea who they were, yet everyone assumed they must be men because their novels are so powerful and original."

"Weren't they men?" Fanny asked in surprise.

"No, they weren't. Everyone was flabbergasted when they turned out to be the daughters of a country clergyman. Their real names were Charlotte, Emily, and Anne Brontë. Sad to say, they're all dead now. I'd be willing to wager that Papa hasn't even heard of the Bells, much less read them."

"Yes," said Elizabeth, "it's true what people say. New ideas take a *very* long time to travel to India. Papa's ideas about women are certainly not new."

Elizabeth wished she could think of an example to disprove Papa's claim that there had never been a great woman painter. Alas, she couldn't. But no matter. She herself would just have to be the first!

"I wonder how the peasants really feel towards Papa," Catherine said thoughtfully. "After all, the Indians are a subject people. And many of the peasants are very poor indeed. It would be natural for them to side *with* the *dacoits* and *against* their English rulers."

"If I am to please Papa, I must practice the piano more constantly," said Fanny, following a different line of thought and earning an approving smile from her mother.

The sisters fell to talking about their plans for the next

day. They had invited the station's teenage girls to see the play they were going to present. It was called *The White Dove of Delhi*. Catherine had written it on her voyage home to India.

Jane was to play the lovely Villette, wife of Captain Rochester Heathcliff, who would be played by Catherine herself. Catherine would also take the role of the villainous *Maharajah* Sauron Chand, and Elizabeth the role of the White Dove.

When Catherine asked her to play a *sepoy*—as the Indian soldiers in the Company's army were called— Fanny, with tears in her eyes, had pleaded, "No, no, forgive me. I cannot, cannot act."

Realizing that Fanny would find it utterly intolerable to appear in men's clothes, even before an all-female audience, Catherine decided that she, Jane, and Elizabeth would simply have to double the smaller parts.

But Fanny was quite helpful as the sisters created costumes out of old curtains and props of pasteboard, paint, and gilt paper. And she eagerly agreed to be the entire stage crew for the production. As the artistic sister, Elizabeth designed the sets.

Having put the finishing touches on the costume to be worn by Captain Heathcliff's horse, the girls prepared for bed.

Their *ayah*, Komal, came with them to lower the mosquito netting around their beds, as she had done every night since Catherine was a baby. The humming of frustrated mosquitoes soon lulled the sisters to sleep.

CHAPTER TWO: CHRISTMAS MORNING

Catherine opened her eyes the next morning to the singing of cicadas and the harsh cawing of peacocks. Sunlight streamed in through the narrow windows. Her mother was standing by the bed, and in her hands were four identical books. Catherine's face brightened at the sight of reading matter.

"Christmas presents after all?" she asked hopefully.

"Well, in a manner of speaking. They are copies of *Pilgrim's Progress*. When Mrs. Brown heard that we weren't going to exchange presents, she gave me one for each of you girls. She was shocked that we don't own the book. The Browns brought copies of it from England to give to their converts, but so far they have converted almost no one. Hindus and Mussulmen do seem to cling to their religion. I can't imagine why."

"What about the converts the Browns *have* made?" asked Fanny, who was now awake. "Has Reverend Brown given the book to them?"

"Oh, they can't read English. Since it has to keep the peace and protect its territory, the Company uses almost all the tax money it collects to pay its *sepoys* and officials. It has little leftover to spend on native schools."

Mrs. May placed a book on each of the beds.

"Why don't you girls stay here and read these for a while?" she suggested. "I must go out for an hour or two. We can have our special Christmas breakfast when I return."

Fanny began to read her book with a strained expression, as if she expected to be tested on its contents.

Elizabeth glanced at the first few pages, closed the volume, and went to her drawing table. Taking out some tubes of paint, she began mixing colors with a palette knife.

Jane dressed carefully and left the room to lay out the breakfast and cut flowers to adorn the table. She sometimes helped with the more ornamental household chores

Catherine opened *Pilgrim's Progress* and was soon deeply absorbed. An hour passed before she closed it.

"Goodness! This is a strange book, Fanny," she exclaimed. "Nothing in the story is what it seems. Everything stands for something else. What do you think it means?"

"Well, I'm pretty sure that the hero, Christian, stands for the soul," Fanny said reverently. "The city he's travelling to stands for heaven. The burdens Christian carries stand for the failings he must get rid of before he can enter the city. So the book is really about how to find salvation."

"Christian thinks that having the right kind of faith is the way you get to heaven," Catherine said, "but I don't agree with him. I think treating other people decently is far more important. Still, the story got me thinking. Good fiction always does that, which is why I want to write novels."

"But a picture is worth a thousand words. Maybe even

two thousand if the words were written by you, Catherine," Elizabeth said tartly, as their mother called out that breakfast was ready.

Fanny slowly followed her sisters from the room. She could feel her sins resting heavily on her shoulders. She tried so hard to live for others, but she never really succeeded.

Mrs. May and Jane were waiting in the dining room. The table was decorated with huge vases of velvety, deep red roses, for even during the cool season, roses grow in India with a tropical abandon unknown in England. Plates of cake and bonbons were artistically arranged on the white tablecloth.

Two tins of Fuller's famously rich walnut cake had been ordered from England several months earlier. This was a tradition in the May family, and the annual Christmas treat was much anticipated by the three younger girls, who had spent their whole lives in India. Today, all four sisters were hungry, for their *chota hazri*, as breakfast was called in British India, had been delayed by their mother's absence.

Elizabeth was reaching for the cake when Mrs. May's fingers closed gently around her wrist.

"Wait just a moment, Lizzie, please. There's something I want to tell you girls before you begin. This morning Komal asked me to visit her cousin, who has just returned from Lucknow and is staying with her."

"Really?" asked Jane excitedly, "Do you mean the legendary Pushpa Ghosh, the Hindu girl who is *legally* married to an English officer?"

"Yes, I do. Mrs. Jennings, as Pushpa should properly be called, is one of the few Indian women who have married Englishmen in recent years. The Company frowns on these mixed-race unions. I'm not sure I approve myself, but once a marriage has been made, it should be sacred, or so I think. Lieutenant Jennings, however, does not agree. When he learned that his regiment was being sent to England, he left Lucknow in secret. Then he wrote Pushpa that he did not want her or their son Mahendra to go with him."

"Oh, how cruel," Fanny cried out.

"It certainly was. The lieutenant told Pushpa that he had fallen in love with a fair-haired English girl and would seek a divorce so he could marry her. Divorce is very expensive, but he has plenty of money. He actually ended his letter by saying, 'I hope this finds you and Mahendra in good health. You will be pleased to hear that I am in tip-top condition at present.'"

Elizabeth rolled her eyes.

"Really," Mrs. May continued, "I sometimes think that men are beyond a woman's comprehension. It's astonishing how little attention they pay to other people's feelings. Look at your Papa. He is obsessed with paperwork and nothing *but* paperwork."

"What will Pushpa do?" Jane asked.

"The Company will not pay Pushpa's fare to England if her husband does not ask them to, so even if she wanted to defy him, she couldn't."

"How cruel," Fanny cried again, and added as an afterthought, "but what has this to do with our *chota hazri?"*

"Pushpa seemed very depressed. She was crying so hard that she couldn't speak to me. But Komal told me what she thinks."

"And what *does* she think?" Catherine asked curiously.

"Pushpa says the English believe that Indian blood is tainted. If a person has one single drop of it, they treat her like an animal. Though it will take time for Pushpa to get over her anger, I thought we could show that we regard her as a true English wife by sharing our walnut cake with her. Pushpa has of course heard of Fuller's from Lieutenant Jennings."

Such a remedy for such an affliction seemed so absurd that the girls were unable to stop themselves from laughing. But surely the gesture could do no harm. They began to pack the breakfast into baskets, for it was a long way to Komal's cottage, and they no longer had a carriage to ride in. Parasols and baskets in hand, the family set out.

Leaving the civil lines, the Mays threaded their way through a maze of narrow lanes. Indians swarmed around them. Some of the men wore elaborate turbans and clean white *dhotis*, as the lengths of cloth wound about their waists were called. The *dhotis* reminded Mrs. May of a baby's nappy, but she kept this thought to herself. Some of the women looked prosperous in brightly colored *saris* or the embroidered trouser suits known as *salwar kameez*, with sparkling bangles on their wrists and ankles.

But most of the Indians they passed were skinny and

ragged. A legless beggar held out an earthenware bowl for alms. Mangy pariah dogs sniffed the garbage in the gutters. An occasional cow wandered by. Mrs. May pressed her skirts closer to her body. Fanny fixed her eyes upon the ground.

Komal's home was small and neat. Mahendra sat on the well-swept floor playing with some brightly painted clay animals. Pushpa stood by, watching him tenderly. Jane was stunned by her beauty. Pushpa had a heavy braid of jet-black hair and big brown eyes. Her green cotton *sari* with its blue border was *very* becoming, though it did reveal rather too much golden skin. Mahendra resembled his mother. Pushpa's eyes were red, but her face was calm.

Komal was stirring a pot of *dal* over a charcoal fire.

Mrs. May explained the reason for her second visit as she unpacked the breakfast. Pushpa seemed to find the idea that walnut cake could heal a broken heart less amusing than the May girls had. She smiled rather grimly.

"I know you mean well, Mrs. May. You have always treated Komal kindly, and she is fond of your family. Because of your kindness, I will share a meal with you and your daughters. But after this day, I shall return to my village and to Indian ways. As Kali is my witness, never again will I have anything to do with foreigners."

The girls gazed at Pushpa, surprised to hear such perfect English issue from an Indian mouth.

"Yes, I can speak like an Englishwoman," Pushpa said, "I lived among the English in Lucknow for years. I fell in love with Lieutenant Jennings when he begged me to marry him. He told me that he would always adore me. Of course, I was flattered to be chosen by an Englishman."

"Yes, indeed," Mrs. May said immediately, "Lieutenant Jennings paid you a great compliment."

"No, it only seemed that way. Accepting his proposal was really a terrible mistake. I left my people for him. I learned to read English as well as to talk it. I almost forgot that I was an Indian."

"How awful that the man you loved should have treated you so cruelly," Jane said sympathetically.

"Yes, and now he tells me that he has fallen in love with a woman who is 'as pure as the driven snow.' I imagine that she is equally cold. My love was as hot as an August day in Lucknow, and in the end he found that embarrassing, because I — "

"Let us sit down to breakfast," Mrs. May interrupted in a stifled voice. It would not be at all suitable for Pushpa to continue in this vein.

Mrs. May had done everything possible to protect the innocence of her daughters. She shuddered as she remembered the shocking paintings that adorned every Hindu temple. Male and female gods intertwined in every imaginable position! The mixture of sensuality and religion was really quite indecent. Whenever they passed a temple, she frantically directed the girls' attention to the inevitable statues of bright blue sacred cows. Of course, it was absurd to think that a cow could be sacred, but at least the blue cows were not doing anything improper. And she had tried to distract the girls whenever they passed natives washing themselves in public. But it had not been easy, except in Fanny's case.

Pushpa smiled bitterly once again and was silent. Fanny tried to lighten the atmosphere by praising the *dal*. Catherine asked Pushpa what it would be like for her to return to her village.

"Our family is of the *kshatriya* or warrior caste and my father is a landowner, a *zamindar*," Pushpa answered, "so we will not starve. But Hindus believe that when a marriage ends, for whatever reason, the wife is to blame. So I will be blamed. Perhaps the villagers will want me to be treated as a widow, to wear a plain, white *sari* and eat only tasteless foods."

"Why on earth would they want you to do that?" Elizabeth asked.

"To show that I am still mourning for my husband as a widow should. Mourning so deeply that I wish for no earthly pleasures! I wonder how many widows really feel that way?"

Mrs. May wondered as well. But she said nothing.

"Fortunately my father is a very enlightened man. He will protect me. Then too, my husband is not actually dead," Pushpa added, "so there will be no question of my having to burn myself on his funeral pyre. Though this custom, *sati*, has been outlawed by the English, it is still sometimes practiced."

"The custom was barbarous," said Elizabeth emphatically, "It is as bad as child marriage. And blaming the wife whenever a marriage goes wrong is terribly unfair."

"*Sati* and child marriage *are* evil customs," Pushpa agreed, "but are English customs so much better? The English pride themselves on treating women well. But when a married couple separates in England, the husband gets to keep their children even if he was the guilty one. He also gets to keep his wife's property!"

"Is that really true?" Elizabeth asked her mother in a startled tone. Mrs. May's silence gave reluctant consent.

"Of course," Pushpa said, "Englishmen can give a long list of reasons why these customs are sensible and necessary, but then Indians are just as well able to defend *sati*. In both countries, prostitution — "

Mrs. May stood up hastily and bundled the remains of the breakfast into a basket. "The girls are giving a play this afternoon. We simply must fly," she said, waving her arms as if she hoped to rise into the air.

Pushpa understood why she had been interrupted.

"Perhaps it is a good thing that Mahin and I are returning to our people," she said in a malicious tone. "This is not a good time to link one's fate to the Company's government, or as Indians call it, its *raj*. The *sepoys* are restless. Many believe that the Company wants to convert India to Christianity by force. Why else, they say, should the country be swarming with missionaries?"

"But surely they are mistaken," Fanny said. "One cannot be made a believer by force. Christianity is a matter of conviction."

"Perhaps so," Pushpa answered, "but an idea may be powerful even if it is mistaken."

The sisters shook Pushpa's hand as they left the room.

Elizabeth remembered how Englishmen would joke with one another, "Never shake hands with a Hindu. You don't know where that hand has been." That was hardly fair. Komal said that her people wiped themselves with their left hands, keeping the right hand exclusively for eating. Which was more than one could say of the English.

As the Mays walked through Komal's garden, they heard the maddening, endlessly repeated cry of the brain fever bird, "Brain fever, *brain fever, BRAIN FEVER.*" And their heads really were spinning from Pushpa's revelations.

"I suppose we shall never see Pushpa again," said Catherine thoughtfully. "And I think that's a pity."

Mrs. May did not regret it.

CHAPTER THREE: THE WHITE DOVE OF DELHI

Catherine had her doubts about the play, even though she was its author. It was based on a novel by a popular Anglo-Indian writer. Catherine thought the story was utterly absurd. But writers should always consider their audience. And given her audience, a tale of British superiority was clearly called for. Perhaps the play would be a success, stupid though it was.

The fact that Catherine had only three actors and one stagehand at her disposal also worried her. But at least she'd been able to give names she liked to the English characters!

The drama was to be performed in the drawing room. A curtain had been rigged up, and a bank of seats created by mounting the second row of chairs on carefully stacked piles of books. As the spectators climbed into their shakily balanced seats, they were warned not to wriggle.

Fanny pulled the curtain aside to reveal a breathtaking scene, which had been conceived and arranged by Elizabeth. Pots of ferns from the veranda and artistically draped green muslin created a sylvan glade. Captain Rochester Heathcliff entered astride a gallant black warhorse. The horse's gait was a bit halting, and its front and back ends both sighed loudly as the captain dismounted.

Freed of its burden, the horse wandered off stage, its rear legs gaining slightly on the front ones.

"Where can my loyal servant Ram Das be keeping

himself?" Captain Heathcliff cried lustily.

After a longish pause, Ram Das raced onstage, hastily tucking in the ends of his *dhoti*, his turban partly unwound. Mrs. May had had her doubts about Elizabeth's appearing either as a horse's behind or as a servant in a *dhoti*. But her daughters had overruled her.

"Ram Das," the captain asked, "where is my wife Villette? She was supposed to meet me here, but she has not yet arrived. Surely no misfortune can have befallen her?"

"Indeed, *Sahib*, thy slave cannot tell thee for sure why thy lady is not here. She rode out this morning from thy bungalow, attended by her groom. Perhaps the groom has betrayed her into the hands of thine enemies," Ram Das answered.

"But the *sepoys* love me," Captain Heathcliff responded. "Surely none of them would allow Villette to come to harm?"

"Even so," Ram Das replied in reverent tones. "Though as an English gentleman thou art too modest to tell the tale, they remember that thou once saved a wounded *sepoy* amid bullets that fell like hail. They say that Heathcliff *Sahib* is a diamond fit for a king's turban, never smiting black men with his foot like other officers."

"Why then should I fear?" the captain asked.

"Because thy wife's groom is a man of low caste, given to all manner of unclean practices. The polluted untouchable whose fate requires him to handle filth will have few scruples about killing a woman."

As Ram Das salaamed humbly, the remainder of his turban unwound itself and a quantity of dark hair tumbled down.

"But who could do evil to my virtuous wife?" Captain Heathcliff demanded. "She is as pure as a newborn kitten."

"Thou speakest truth," Ram Das replied. "But many black men covet white-skinned women. This is only too true of *Maharajah* Sauron Chand, and thy groom may be the instrument of his foul desires. The *Maharajah's* harem is filled with women of many colors, shapes, and sizes."

Captain Heathcliff staggered backwards, smiting his brow. "My horse, my horse immediately, Ram Das," he cried in agitated tones.

Ram Das disappeared into the dining room, and after a while, the horse strolled onstage alone. Elizabeth was playing *both* the horse *and* Ram Das, and she couldn't play them simultaneously.

Heathcliff mounted, and the horse struggled painfully offstage. Fanny drew the curtain to thunderous applause. Act One was over.

The spectators in the upper row of seats climbed down gingerly. Mrs. May could be heard telling Mrs. Brown in apologetic tones that although the play's subject matter was a bit shocking, it was really a highly moral work.

Act Two was set in the *Maharajah's* harem, which was gorgeously decorated with Christmas tree ornaments that the Mays had purchased in more prosperous times. Seen from a distance, they twinkled and glowed like real jewels. Mrs. May's best cashmere shawl adorned a divan on which Villette Heathcliff was seated, sobbing bitterly.

Maharajah Sauron Chand entered, his tall figure momentarily darkening the doorway from the dining room. His face was unevenly streaked with purplish dye.

"Beautiful woman, thou art mine," he told Villette. "If thou comest to me of thine own free will, I shall shower thee with jewels. But if thou shouldst resist me, then thy fate shall not be so pleasant."

He winked suggestively.

"Can nothing move you?" Villette cried. "Do you not fear God? Are you not afraid of the golden-haired *Rani*, your father's adopted daughter, whom men call the White Dove of Delhi? She will allow no cruel deeds to be done in these dominions."

"Beautiful woman," the *Maharajah* repeated, with an exceptionally foul leer. "The White Dove knows not that thou art here. She cannot save three. Wilt thou not *now* consent?"

Villette rose from the divan.

"I believe implicitly in God," she said, gazing piously at the chandelier. "And though I hold suicide to be a dastardly sin, I will take my own life rather than be polluted by your unclean hands."

Here she drew a large kitchen knife from beneath her robes and aimed the point at her breast.

"I would not stain my husband's British honor for all the gold in India."

Again, she flourished the knife, but the *Maharajah* suddenly sprang towards her and twisted it from her grasp.

With a piteous cry, Villette sank gracefully to the ground. As the *Maharajah* approached her, the audience gasped.

At this exciting moment, the White Dove of Delhi entered, wearing a wig of yellow yarn.

Mrs. May thought the wig made Lizzie look like an animated dust mop. It was almost as bad as the *dhoti* she had worn in the previous act.

"Evil brother," the White Dove declaimed, gazing at Sauron Chand with a severe expression, "our father did not trust you. And so when he died, he left his armies under my command, though I am only his foster daughter. I shall save this woman. Soldiers, seize Sauron Chand."

Because Jane, Catherine, and Elizabeth were all onstage, no one remained to represent the army whose aid the White Dove was demanding.

So Fanny drew the curtain as hastily as possible. From behind it, Sauron Chand could be heard crying loudly, "Oh, the soldiers are here! Oh, they have arrested me!"

With this brilliant *coup de théâtre*, the second act ended.

Refreshments were to be served during the interval. Anticipating this treat, the spectators jumped eagerly to their feet. The stacks of books toppled over, and the girls went down in a heap of muslin.

Legs waved in the air. "Help me someone, my unmentionables are showing!" Susan Brown cried loudly.

But no one was hurt, and soon they were enjoying an excellent tea. Mrs. May often said that too much should not be expected from Indian servants. Their brains were not properly developed. That was why she allowed the cook to serve Indian sweets instead of asking him to make European pastries. His *gulab jamun*, a sort of cottage cheese ball soaked in syrup, and his *ras malai*, a sort of cottage cheese patty floating in cardamom flavored cream sauce, were especially delicious.

"I must say the Indians do wonderful things with cottage cheese," commented plump Ellen Barnfather.

Jane thought the comment quite superfluous. But then, Ellen was always talking about food. Her excessive interest in it stuck out like a sore thumb... or like Susan's Brown's shiny red nose.

Fortified, the audience returned to their seats, whose base of books had been painstakingly reconstructed by Fanny. Though she had been forced to skip tea, Fanny welcomed the chance to sacrifice a merely physical pleasure for the good of others.

Act Three was set in the drawing room of the Heathcliffs' bungalow. When the curtain opened, Captain Heathcliff, his wife, and the White Dove were all seated, drinking real tea and eating real toast.

Watching from offstage, Fanny realized that the cook had had to prepare two different teas, one for the audience and one for the scene which was now being acted. That was rather hard lines on him. Someone should surely have remembered the poor cook, even if they hadn't remembered Fanny.

"My angel wife," Heathcliff exclaimed, "I feel my manhood returning now that I no longer fear you might suffer the fate worse than death."

"Yes, husband," Villette said, "we owe our happiness to the White Dove. I feel strangely drawn to her."

"How does it happen," Heathcliff asked the Dove, "that you were living as the daughter of the late *Maharajah*?"

"Sixteen years ago," she said sweetly, "a peasant woman named Vijaylakshmi brought a newborn baby to the *Maharajah*. She asked him to adopt it and died before he could answer. But he agreed, for his heart yearned towards the child. I was that baby."

"Vijaylakshmi! Sixteen years ago!" Villette exclaimed. "Oh, all-powerful God, you have restored my lost sister."

Her husband and the Dove looked at her in surprise.

"Yes, it is even so," Villette continued. "Sixteen years ago, my parents set out on a journey, leaving me behind. The child my mother expected was not yet due. But while my father was hunting, their camp was attacked by *dacoits*. The servants fled, for the Hindu has little staying power. When the servants came back, my mother was lying dead in her tent. They covered her up. When my father returned, he could not bear to look upon her body. He buried her in her coverings, believing that he was burying her unborn child along with her."

"And you think... ?" the Dove said breathlessly.

"Yes, I see now that a living child was born. My mother must have died from terror, and Vijaylakshmi fled with the infant. You are that infant. The longing I felt when first I saw you was the call of race to kindred race."

"My sister," the White Dove cried. The two actresses then fainted alternately on the divan, which was not quite large enough to hold them both.

"Dove," Captain Heathcliff concluded, "it does not surprise me to learn that you are an English lady by birth, for you have always acted like one."

Fanny drew the curtain.

After taking their bows, the actresses mingled with the audience. Susan Brown thought the play beautiful and uplifting. She was especially touched by Villette's unshakeable faith in God.

"Her faith may seem admirable to you," Elizabeth said, "but I'm not sure it makes much sense to kill yourself to avoid rape. Doubtless rape is a very unpleasant experience, but even after such an experience life is worth living. On the whole, I thought it was a stupid play."

"I thought it was utterly absurd," Catherine said, "though I am technically the author. All the ideas came from the novel. They're definitely not mine. But I'm glad Susan found the play moving, because that's what I was aiming at."

"I don't think the play was stupid at all," Susan

responded, somewhat startled at having to defend it against its author. "The character of Ram Das showed that the best type of native is devoted to his European masters. That is nothing more than the simple truth."

"Yes, indeed," said Ellen Barnfather. "And we all know that natives are attracted to English women, though of course it isn't nice to say so in public."

"Are they really?" Fanny said anxiously, racking her brains for an example of such attraction.

"Certainly they are," Susan responded in satisfied tones.

Noticing that Susan's nose was glowing even more brightly than usual, Jane sent God a quick message of thanks for her own pretty face. She must have looked awfully nice dressed up as Villette Heathcliff. Yes, amateur theatricals were *very* enjoyable!

"I've read some English novels about India," Elizabeth said, "and the Indian characters always talk the same funny kind of English. Lots of 'thees' and 'thous,' as if they're living in the Middle Ages. It's supposed to show that they're really speaking Hindi. But it just makes them sound backward."

"In the novel, the White Dove speaks perfect English, even though she was raised by Indians," Catherine said. "Apparently she got both good morals *and* good diction from her pure English blood. But there are plenty of people in England whose grammar is just awful—and their morals are even worse. I lived there for eight years and I know."

CHAPTER FOUR: THE DANCE

A few weeks after Christmas, Jane ran into the drawing room where Fanny and Catherine were sitting. Fanny was sewing briskly and humming *What a Friend We Have in Jesus*. Catherine's needle moved languidly.

"Catherine! Such fun! Only see!" Jane cried. "Here's a regular note of invitation from Mrs. Beaglehole for tomorrow night. The Beagleholes give the *best* parties. All the officers from the cantonment come and the refreshments are incredible."

"What kind of party?" Catherine asked warily. She hated dances, but she kept her feelings to herself. It was bad enough that she had always been a wallflower in England — but it would be too shaming to admit it.

"Oh, a dance, to be sure." Jane loved dances. "It begins at eight and ends with supper at eleven. The invitation is addressed to 'Miss May and Miss Jane May.' Isn't that elegant? Now what on earth shall we wear?"

"What's the use of asking that when you know we have only one party dress each?" Catherine said irritably.

"Well, accessories..."

"You haven't seen my dress yet, Jane. Mama told me to have it made while I was still in England. So it's the latest mode — green silk with a bustle. The problem is that I wore it to a ball in London, and I have this trick of standing with my back quite close to the fire. It's utterly freezing in England. So I scorched the bustle. I didn't realize how far it stuck out! The dress has been mended, but the burn still shows."

Catherine did not add that on that painful occasion, she had been without a partner for three dances in a row. She had grown chilly from sitting still and had gone to the fireplace to warm up.

"That is unfortunate," said Jane, who always kept her clothing in perfect order. "But you must simply spend as much time as possible pressed against the wall, so the back of your dress won't show. You must simply turn down *all* your invitations to dance."

Catherine smiled. Jane wanted her to be a wallflower in the most literal sense of the term. Would she really have to turn down any invitations to achieve this goal? Maybe not.

But in British India there were far more men than women. In England it was just the opposite. So she *might* be asked to dance at the Beagleholes' party. But then, she hated dancing, oh *too* utterly... so it was comforting to think that if she *were* asked, she had a perfect reason for saying no.

"I shall wear my blue sprigged muslin, of course," Jane continued. "It's not quite new, and it certainly looks like the work of a *durzi*, which unfortunately it is. But I have some new blue slippers to go with it, and I shall wear fresh flowers in my hair. Roses, I think. I have been very careful of my white kid gloves, and they are still nice."

"My gloves have ink on them. I had a fabulous idea for a story just as I was going out, so I wrote it down without bothering to take them off. My pen spluttered and now they are utterly spotted, but frankly, I don't care. Art comes first."

"Does it indeed?" Jane asked, in the tone of one who feels herself criticized.

"Birds in their little nests agree," said Fanny, making a wry face.

The next evening saw Jane and Catherine dressing for the dance under their mother's watchful eye. They refused her suggestion that they wear cork spine protectors and tie a length of flannel around their hips to protect the "organs peculiar to the female sex" from catching a chill.

"If you insist," Mrs. May conceded reluctantly, "but that is the only compromise I shall make. Dressing well is a duty, not a pleasure. A lady must wear clothing that is suited to her station. Appropriate clothes show that one has a proper sense of social boundaries. Then too, girls should always be nice and tidy in their dress."

"Fanny is tidy," said Elizabeth, who was looking on. "As a matter of fact, my nickname for her is 'Lady Tidy.' Jane usually looks nice, but you wouldn't exactly call her tidy. Too many frills and furbelows. Catherine is almost always a mess."

"And what about you?" Catherine shot back.

"Oh, I dress with quiet propriety," said Elizabeth ironically. "I have a horror of being over trimmed. That's another way of saying that I pay just enough attention to my clothes to keep Mama from getting *too* upset."

"If only you would do the same, Catherine," Mrs. May said gently.

Jane stood up in a calico camisole and lisle thread

stockings supported by fancy knitted garters. Over the stockings, she slipped on ankle length drawers. Over the camisole, she laced a very serious corset, reinforced with whalebone.

She held her breath while Mrs. May tugged the strings.

Over the corset, Jane buttoned on a cotton petticoat bodice, delicately embroidered. Around her waist, she fastened a strong white flannel petticoat, hooped with steel. Over this went two fine cotton petticoats, the first plain, the second trimmed with lace.

On her feet, she wore her high-heeled evening slippers, on her hands, the white kid gloves.

Only now was Jane ready to slip into her gown, which had twelve yards of fabric in its ruffled skirt.

Catherine's dress was similar to Jane's, except for the bustle. She insisted on wearing flat shoes.

Elizabeth had once asked her mother why they had to wear so much clothing in such a hot climate. Daytime temperatures were quite warm even during the so-called cold weather.

"It isn't exactly necessary," Mrs. May replied, "but no nice girl would want men to see the shape of her legs."

Mrs. May told Catherine and Jane to wear cloaks for the walk to the party and grew agitated when they said that they were already broiling hot. Her daughters took pity on her. Would she survive the disgrace if they appeared out of doors with bare arms? Probably not. They wrapped themselves up as directed.

The Residency, where the Beagleholes lived, was

located at the opposite end of the civil lines from the Mays' home. The walk was quite long, and the sisters felt breathless by the time they got there. The sheer weight of their clothing was almost overwhelming. The tight corsets didn't help.

The *khansama* conducted them to the ballroom, which was brightly lighted by dozens of expensive wax candles in graceful brass sconces. The polished dance floor gleamed invitingly. The chairs set out for the chaperones, upholstered in figured pink damask, were reflected in the floor as if in a mirror. Servants rushed about. As the most important Company official in Shivapur, Mr. Beaglehole could afford the best of everything.

The regimental band was playing *The Girl I Left Behind Me*. Catherine thought of Pushpa. Jane experienced a moment of pure joy.

Every girl at the ball was given a small program, with a tiny pencil suspended from a loop of ribbon. The program listed polkas, reels, waltzes, in their prescribed order. There was a space beside each dance where you could write the name of the man you'd promised it to. Jane's program was soon black with names.

The dancing began. A handsome officer quickly whirled Jane onto the dance floor, while Catherine pressed her back firmly against the wall. To her surprise, she received several invitations to dance, but she rejected them all. Her program remained blank. Thank heaven, her scorched gown was protecting her from her personal version of a "fate worse than death" — dancing with strangers.

Still, it was upsetting to have to say "no" again and again, so Catherine backed into a curtained recess as a short, stout man approached her with a determined expression. Unfortunately, another bashful person had chosen the same refuge. As the curtain fell behind her, Catherine found herself facing a dark-skinned Indian boy about her own age, wearing well-cut European evening clothes and an orchid in his buttonhole.

"Goodness, who are you?" she asked in surprise.

"Do you mean, what am I doing here?" the boy countered in a tone that was neither quite hostile nor quite pleasant.

And indeed this *was* what Catherine wanted to know, for the boy was the only Indian at the gathering. It was utterly unusual for Indians to be invited to English parties.

"Well, yes," said Catherine, who was incurably honest, "but that doesn't mean I'm unhappy to see you. I've just come back to Shivapur from London, and I find the society here a bit limited. I'm only too glad to meet someone different."

"That's better than nothing," the boy said, smiling. "So I'll tell you that my name is Mahmud Ali. You can call me Ali."

"Mahmud Ali! Then you must be the son of the ruler of Malior. His title is *Nawab*, isn't it? I've heard quite a bit about Malior since I returned. It's not far from Shivapur and is an independent state, though the Company would like to take it over. The ruling family are

Mussulmen. Isn't that right?"

"You're right about Malior, but wrong about me. I'm the *Nawab*'s grandson, not his son. Both my parents are dead. And you are Catherine May. I've seen you with your sisters during the last few weeks. My tutor, Mr. James Keats, knows your family. He's told me about all of you, but especially about your sister Jane."

"I hope you haven't heard anything bad about *me*," Catherine said, laughing. "Unlike Jane, I haven't yet learned how to be a proper *memsahib*, and perhaps I never will. But you haven't told me how you happened to be invited to this party *or* why you're hiding in an alcove. I'm hiding because my gown is scorched. Jane said I must keep my back to the wall to hide the burned place. I generally feel that I've got my back to the wall at dances in any case."

"I haven't heard much about *you* specifically," Ali said bluntly, "But before I explain why I was invited, I want to ask you a question. Do you know that there is unrest in the country?"

"Yes, I know some people think there might be trouble. We've been worried about Papa, because he is out in the countryside. But here in Shivapur, even if some *sepoys* do mutiny, Papa says that most will stay loyal, and they will protect us. Surely there can be no real danger?"

"Have you heard about the *chapattis*?"

"Nothing at all. Isn't a *chapatti* a kind of flatbread?"

"Yes, it's baked on a griddle," Ali said. "Lately strangers have been appearing in villages and giving *chapattis* to the village headmen. No one knows what it means, but some villagers think the bread comes from the Company and is a sign that it will soon force Indians to share the food of Christians. Since Christians eat pork and beef, neither Mussulmen nor Hindus can share their food without violating sacred laws. The villagers say that after they have violated these laws, they will have no religion. Then the Company can make them become Christians."

"I have heard some rumors about forced conversions. But surely the idea that the Company would send *chapattis* to hint at its intentions is utterly absurd?"

"I think the rumor is false," Ali said thoughtfully, "but it's not completely absurd. The English have interfered with many Indian customs. The country is swarming with missionaries who think Hindus are benighted idol worshippers and Mussulmen are lustful polygamists. The missionaries' goal *is* to convert us, though of course they won't do it with *chapattis*."

"How do you explain the *chapattis*, then?" Catherine asked.

"In my opinion, Indians who want to throw the British out of our country are the ones sending the *chapattis* around. The same Indians have started the rumors. They probably think the people will rebel if they feel their religion is threatened."

"But surely the appearance of mysterious bits of bread isn't enough to make them feel that it is!"

"Well, that's not the only reason why many Indians are worried about their religion," Ali said.

He explained that the *sepoys* were already upset about the new Enfield rifles when the *chapatti* business started. In order to load an Enfield rifle, the *sepoy* had to bite off the end of the cartridge and pour the gunpowder from the cartridge into the barrel.

"The grease in the cartridge touches the soldier's lips when he bites it," Ali concluded. He sounded quite agitated.

"That must be unpleasant," Catherine said in a puzzled tone, "but *sepoys* have to do so many unpleasant things. Why should they get hysterical about this particular one?"

"Because the grease was a mixture of pork and beef fat, that's why. Touching it to their lips defiled both Mussulmen and Hindus. Though the army is now letting them to make grease from ghee and beeswax, the *sepoys* will not forget. They loathe the new rifles."

"That's alarming, to be sure, but perhaps it will all blow over. And you still haven't told me why you were invited to this party. Can the *chapattis* have anything to do with it?"

"Actually, they're the whole explanation. Mr. Beaglehole is more alarmed by the state of the country than you seem to be. My grandfather commands the army of Malior. It's not much of an army, but still *it is* an army of sorts. Mr. Beaglehole wants to be sure of my grandfather's loyalty if there is trouble. So he invited me to his party. As it happens, I hate parties."

"Then why did you come?"

"My grandfather insisted. *He* believes that if a rebellion

flares up, the English will win. God is on the side of the big battalions, my grandfather says, and the English have lots of money and modern weapons. So he wants me to stay in Mr. Beaglehole's good books."

"God is on the side of the big battalions!" Catherine said. "I like that phrase. I wish I could write it down. I want to be a writer. I usually carry a notebook, but Jane would never let me bring it to a dance. She doesn't think much of my manners. She's going to raise her eyebrows if she sees me doing anything that embarrasses her."

"You want to be a writer? So do I. A poet, to be precise. India has a long tradition of poetry in Sanskrit and Persian."

Ali looked so rapturous that Catherine feared he was about to recite some of his own verse. It was sure to be in a language she did not understand. But she realized that meeting him had turned the party from an ordeal into a pleasure. If he started spouting Sanskrit, she would bear it... womanfully. She was pleased with the word. A moment later, she peeked out through the curtains and caught a fleeting glimpse of her sister.

Jane was dancing with Lieutenant Palliser for the third time. The lieutenant was so handsome, so tall. He looked so manly in his uniform. Jane was glad that this number was a waltz, for the lieutenant was an excellent walzer and so was she. As she looked up into his green eyes, they whirled smoothly around the floor. Jane's wide skirts billowed. She could feel the lieutenant's hand resting on her waist. Could anything be more delightful than this very waltz? Could anything be more elegant than this very ball?

When the waltz ended, Lieutenant Palliser politely conducted Jane to a seat. He took her fan from her hand and worked it away, as if for dear life. She gazed at him dreamily as the air cooled her forehead. They were both too short of breath to say much.

"Many thanks, dear lady... my pleasure... so grateful..." Lieutenant Palliser gasped. He bent over Jane's hand and touched his lips to her spotless glove.

Then the band started up again, and Jane's next partner, James Keats, came to claim her. A nice young man, Jane thought, though he was neither as tall as the lieutenant, nor as handsome. And of course he wasn't wearing a uniform. She had met him several times at Shivapur parties, and she knew he liked her. She felt sure he had asked her for this particular dance because it was the last one before supper would be served. Your partner for that dance was supposed to sit next to you at supper, as he very well knew.

James Keats put an arm around Jane and they moved onto the floor. Jane enjoyed his admiring gaze, but oh, if only he were a better dancer. Trying to do the polka with him was nerve racking. And sure enough, they had barely circled the room once, when he took a false step and kicked the side of her foot quite powerfully. The high-heeled slipper twisted under her and a sharp pain shot up her leg. She barely saved herself from falling, as she gave a cry of anguish.

Mr. Keats looked at her in horror. Jane thought he would be awfully humiliated if she told him that he had caused her injury. She decided to protect his masculine pride. After all, he hadn't meant to hurt her.

"Oh, Mr. Keats," she said softly, "I'm afraid I have sprained my ankle. How clumsy of me. It was the slippers. I had no idea they'd be so hard to dance in. I can't dance any more, so let's join my sister. She's over in that alcove."

James Keats helped Jane hobble off the dance floor. Once inside the alcove, she sank into a chair without introducing him.

Catherine couldn't help raising her eyebrows dramatically. The chance to correct her proper sister was too good to miss.

Jane took the hint. "Mr. Keats, this is my sister Catherine May, just returned from England. Catherine, this is Mr. James Keats," she said. She told the story of her accident, concealing James's role in it once again.

Catherine introduced Ali to Jane, who seemed even more surprised to see him at the party than she herself had been.

"How does it happen that you are wearing European clothes? Where is your *dhoti*?" Jane blurted.

"I'm a *Mussulman*," Ali said. "Mahmud Ali isn't a Hindu name, and only Hindu men wear *dhotis*. Can you really have spent your whole life in India without noticing that? How very British of you!"

Catherine raised her eyebrows again. Jane gave a little moan of embarrassment, and Mr. Keats gazed at her with an expression of sympathy better suited to a fatal disease than to a social gaffe or even a twisted ankle.

Ali thought his tutor looked absolutely besotted. He cleared his throat.

"My grandfather," he said, "expects the English to rule India for a long while. They despise people who don't understand their ways, so he hired Mr. Keats to give me an English education. He insists that I dress like this whenever I meet Europeans. And he doesn't want me to write poetry, especially not in my own language."

"That sounds a bit confusing," Catherine said.

"Yes, there are times when I hardly know who I am," Ali said. "And I don't think the English *sahibs* really do respect Indians who imitate them. They say we look like dressed up monkeys when we wear European clothing. Don't write that in your notebook, Miss May."

Catherine's heart warmed toward this thoughtful boy.

"I certainly won't," she said. "I don't think it's clever, and I only jot down clever remarks. But if it makes you feel any better, my father doesn't want me to be a writer either. He calls me a 'little woman' and expects me to become a wife and mother. Ugh."

"My grandfather wants me to learn diplomacy and save Malior from being taken over by the Company. An admirable aim, but it's just not *my* aim."

"I feel the same way about being a mother," Catherine said, with a smile. Were she and Elizabeth, caught between their parents' values and their own ambitions, any less confused than Ali? Probably not. Jane and Fanny were a different matter, of course.

At this point, the four were summoned to supper. Since Jane could not squeeze her swollen foot into her slipper, Catherine suggested that she walk to the dining room in her stocking feet. Her floor length skirts would conceal this offense against good breeding.

As custom demanded, Mrs. Beaglehole sent her guests into the dining room in descending order of importance. As an army officer and the son of a baronet, Lieutenant Palliser ranked much higher than James Keats, who was merely the employee of a native ruler. Limping out of the ballroom, Jane saw the lieutenant's tall figure far ahead of her in the line of guests and felt a twinge of envy for his partner, who happened to be Susan Brown. She wasn't pleased that Susan had triumphed over her, even momentarily.

But the supper was terrific. There was actually chocolate ice cream, made with ice shipped all the way from Wenham Lake in the northern United States and stored in the Beagleholes' ice-house, packed in sawdust.

In the dining room, James Keats tore his gaze painfully from Jane's lovely face and forced himself to talk to Catherine, who was sitting on his other side. He feared that it would harm Jane's reputation if he paid her too much attention. But soon he found that he was enjoying himself, for he and Catherine discovered that they both loved the Bells' novels. When he said that *Wuthering Heights* was "simply magnificent," Catherine beamed at him.

Jane was glad that Ali was sitting by Catherine and *not* by her. He seemed like a nice boy, but she preferred her own countrymen. It wouldn't be proper to flirt with an Indian, and she did so enjoy flirting. Since James was talking to Catherine, Jane turned to chat with her other neighbor, a young Company official who always had a lot to say.

Before the May girls left the party, Catherine invited Ali to visit at their bungalow.

"What will Mama say to that?" Jane asked, as the sisters climbed into the Beagleholes' handsome carriage, which had been lent them in consideration of Jane's sprained ankle.

"I'll cross that bridge when I come to it," Catherine said.

CHAPTER FIVE: A CRISIS

There was consternation in the bungalow. The Mays had just finished their *chota hazri* when Komal came to say that the *dhobi* who did their laundry had disappeared. Komal thought he had been upset by the rumors of approaching trouble and had fled to avoid it.

But it was Monday, the day for doing the weekly wash. Since the Mays had been economizing on clothes for some time, they didn't have enough clean garments to last much longer.

"The situation is dire," Fanny said anxiously. "The wash *must* be done. Oh, what are we going to do?"

"I have no idea," Mrs. May answered, looking bewildered. "I have never washed my own clothes. I wouldn't know how to begin, though I suppose one would have to begin with water in some form, wouldn't one?"

"That seems reasonable," Elizabeth said.

"Even when I lived in England, I had a servant to wash the clothes. And of course, in India, there has always been the *dhobi*. Perfectly respectable dresses look like dishcloths when he finishes with them. But if you want your clothes washed in India, it has to be done by a *dhobi*."

"I have heard," Elizabeth said, "that *dhobis* sometimes rent out the dresses that they have taken home with them to wash. They rent them to mixed race girls who can't afford European clothing. Perhaps they see nothing wrong with this practice, but it's unsanitary, to say the least."

"Yes, and it may well be the cause of *dhobi* itch," Jane said shuddering. "*Dhobi* itch is a horrible kind of rash. Thank heaven we've never caught it, but Susan Brown did. I visited her when she had it, and she looked so spotty, like a piece of raisin pudding—*with* a red nose poking out of it."

"Jane!" Fanny exclaimed, in a shocked tone. This was her usual response to Jane's remarks on the subject of Susan Brown's nose. Her sister's vanity distressed her.

"All things considered," Catherine said, "the *dhobi* doesn't sound like much of a loss. Why don't we try doing the wash ourselves? The copy of *Mrs. Seaton's Compete British Housekeeper* that Mama brought from England will tell us what to do. We can learn as we go along. I feel certain that with Mrs. Seaton's wise aid, we can do a *much* better job than the *dhobi*."

"Oh, yes," said Fanny enthusiastically. "And we can save the *dhobi*'s wages, as well as the wear and tear on our clothing. The *dhobi* doesn't make much money, but clothing is very expensive. Papa will be so pleased when he comes back. Not just about the money, but because we're learning a womanly skill. And Mama need not help. She can go out and pay calls."

Mrs. May was relieved. The thought of learning to do housework at her age was not appealing. Supervising her Indian servants was as much as she could contemplate.

Elizabeth took *Mrs. Seaton's Complete British Housekeeper* from the shelf and consulted the index. Soon the sisters were studying the chapter on laundry.

"The first thing to be done," Elizabeth said, "is to sort the clothes. Towels, sheets, tablecloths, body linen— that means underwear, I think—shirts, petticoats, and nightgowns have to be separated from delicate items and from very dirty things like dishcloths. That sounds fairly straightforward."

Once the clothes had been sorted, Jane read aloud: "'Next, examine each stain and decide how to remove it. Both the type of stain and the fabric must be taken into consideration. Ink stains'—that's you, Catherine— 'should be treated with lemon juice, while oil stains must be rubbed with stale bread.'"

"Ink stains are easy to identify," Catherine said good-humoredly, "especially on *my* dresses. But I wouldn't be able to tell an oil stain from any other kind."

"Nor would I," Jane said, "and what I just read you is only the beginning of the section on stains. It goes on and on. 'Wax from candles should be removed by applying a hot coal wrapped in linen.' This is far too complicated. I vote that we just ignore this step. Maybe the regular washing will get rid of the worst stains."

Elizabeth and Catherine agreed in hopeful tones. Fanny remained silent. She was no optimist.

"The next thing to do," Jane said, consulting the book, "is to soak the sheets and suchlike in lukewarm water mixed with soda. While they're soaking, we must dunk the dirtiest items in a solution of lime and water, strain them, and rinse them in a new lime solution. A short soak in plain water will do for the delicate pieces, thank heaven."

The sisters scurried to finish this part of the ritual, which involved several tiring trips to the well and took some time.

"Now," Elizabeth summarized, picking up *Mrs. Seaton* once again, "we are supposed to heat water in something called 'the copper.' It's a device they have in England. The illustration shows a sort of metal barrel with a lid and an enclosed fire. It holds a lot of water. Since we haven't got one, we'll have to boil water in pots on the stove."

After lugging enough water to fill all the large vessels the family possessed, the girls dropped thankfully into chairs. When the water finally boiled, they staggered to their feet, feeling only partially recovered.

As Catherine struggled to lift the largest pot, water slopped over the side, splashing onto the open fire of the charcoal stove. Soot flew into the air and drifted down, sullying the sisters' clothing and the water they had just heated.

"Great God," Catherine wailed, clutching her hair in a dramatic gesture.

"Don't swear, Catherine," Fanny said automatically, looking as if she was about to cry. "Mama wouldn't like it."

Catherine pulled herself together. "The water *is* a bit dirty now, but it's still water, so we must just use it and ignore the soot."

No one disagreed.

As directed by *Mrs. Seaton*, Jane ladled water from the pots onto the soaked sheets and linens and beat them with a wooden stick. Groaning loudly, the girls wrung out the water. They had never imagined a sheet could be so heavy.

"Believe it or not, that was only the pre-wash. Next, it's time for the actual wash. We're supposed to take a bar of soap and dissolve it in boiling water to make a sort of jelly," Elizabeth said, consulting the book.

The sisters rubbed the jelly through the laundry they had just wrung out, transforming it into a huge soapy mountain.

Elizabeth returned to *Mrs. Seaton*. "Oh my heavens, this is really beyond horrible. *Now* we're supposed to rinse off the suds and then rub the things *again* with the jelly. After that, we rinse them, then boil them for *an hour and a half*, then rinse them *again* in boiling water, and *again* in cold water. The cold water should have blue dye in it because soap tends to yellow the whites."

"Yes," said Fanny sadly, taking the book from her sister, "and that's just what we need to do to finish with the sheets and towels—what we're supposed to do with the delicate things and the really dirty ones is even more complicated. And then we need to iron everything. That's a lot of work too. Well, we must simply forge ahead."

"We must do no such thing," said Catherine decisively. "I am too utterly exhausted. I simply can't go on."

"I used to like watching the *dhobi*," Fanny said.

She remembered how he would take the laundry down

to the bathing steps by the river, rub each piece with a bar of soap, and slap it against the rocks. Then he waded out into the current where the flowing water rinsed it. He would dry it by spreading it on the bushes. Perhaps these methods were better suited to India than *Mrs. Seaton's*.

At this moment, Mrs. May returned from her round of calls, neatly dressed, her hair combed smoothly into a bun. She gazed at her daughters with consternation.

"Goodness, girls, you look as if you've been shearing sheep," she exclaimed.

"Yes, we're covered with suds," Jane said, "plus quite a bit of soot. We'll have to wash the dresses we've got on before we can wear them again. And they were fine when we started—except for Catherine's, of course. All we've done so far is make more work."

"Elizabeth," Mrs. May commanded, "Go immediately and tell Komal to hire a new *dhobi*!"

CHAPTER SIX: THE PALACE

"Ali has not kept his promise to visit us," Jane told Catherine one morning in February.

"You mean James Keats has not come to visit *you*," her sister said, smiling. "Komal heard that Ali has a touch of fever. He's confined to his room, and Mr. Keats *has* to stay with him."

Jane looked relieved, but remained silent.

"The Malior Palace isn't teribly far away," Catherine added. "We could borrow some horses from the Barnfathers and ride there one morning to see how Ali is getting along."

Jane knew she should refuse. Mama would certainly disapprove of their calling on two young men. And Mama understood what was proper for a young lady to do. But then it would be such fun to go riding with her sisters and to see James Keats's admiring eyes again.

"Mama will never agree," she said wistfully.

"Mama need never know. We'll leave Fanny at home to take care of her, and we'll say we're riding in the opposite direction."

After much hesitation, Jane decided to go along.

The next day saw Catherine, Jane, and Elizabeth riding toward Malior. The weather was growing warmer, and the girls' path led them through green fields of springing millet and yellow fields of mustard. Behind the fields they could see long swathes of dense, tangled jungle. To Catherine, whose eye was accustomed to the widely spaced old trees that dotted the English countryside, this jungle appeared threatening and utterly impenetrable.

The girls rode past a mud brick village where small thatched huts surrounded a central tank.

Catherine waved at the ragged peasants drawing water from the tank, but most of them did not respond. They stared at the sisters with an expression that she could not read.

Catherine remembered the rumors Ali had told her about. She felt a sharp stab of fear at the thought of her father deep in this hostile countryside. She wished he weren't so sure that the peasants adored him. Then he might stop thinking about his paperwork and pay some attention to his safety.

After an hour's ride, the sisters arrived at the *Nawab's* palace, a large gray stone structure, flanked by soaring minarets. A servant in a red and gold uniform showed them into the audience hall. Its high ceiling was supported by intricately carved pillars, and its floor was covered with resplendent carpets. Blue tiles from Turkey decorated the walls.

Elizabeth couldn't help staring. She had never seen such a lovely room. She had an excellent memory for visual detail, so she hoped she would remember exactly what the hall looked like when she got home. She was dying to paint it.

The *Nawab* himself came forward to receive them. He was a fat, white-bearded old man, whose shrewd face was overshadowed by a jeweled turban. He salaamed gracefully and the sisters curtseyed.

Catherine said they had heard Ali was ill and had come to visit him.

The *Nawab* told them that Ali's illness was not serious. A servant would take them to see his grandson, but first they must visit the room that he had specially furnished in the "English style."

Proudly, he led the way to a parlor crammed with European furniture. There were two upright pianos, three big sofas upholstered in flowered chintz, four elaborately carved armchairs, and a round table with a lamp suspended over it. Red flocked paper covered the walls, heavy green velvet curtains the windows. There was hardly an inch of unoccupied floor space.

Catherine thought the room was like a parody of the dark, overfurnished parlors she had often seen in England. Elizabeth looked around her in horror. This room was as ugly as the audience hall was beautiful!

"Is it not comfortable, handsome, and truly civilized?" the *Nawab* asked. He sounded a bit doubtful. They made polite noises. He smiled and told the servant to take them to Ali's quarters.

Ali was lying on a pile of gorgeous silk cushions. James Keats was sitting on a chair with a book. He shot into the air like a rocket at the sight of Jane.

"We have ridden over to cheer you up, Ali, since you can't come to see us just now," Catherine said. Without waiting for an answer, she pursued the subject that interested her most. "What have you and Mr. Keats been reading?"

"My grandfather wouldn't be too pleased if he knew,

but we've been reading Persian poetry."

"Why wouldn't he?" Elizabeth asked. "It seems like a perfectly respectable subject."

"He wants me to study Latin, not Persian. Like upper class boys do in England. I have learned some, but it doesn't interest me. *Dulce et decorum est pro patria mori.* That means 'it is sweet and fitting to die for one's country.' To an Indian that sounds ridiculous."

"Why so?" Jane asked. "It's a very noble sentiment."

"Of course it is. But Indians don't have a country to die for. The same Englishmen who teach this noble sentiment to their sons have stolen *our* country. What are they but hypocrites?"

"Steady on," Catherine said in a startled tone. "Isn't that unfair? We have brought civilization to India. We're building canals and railways. We're keeping the peace."

"Yes," Jane added, "and we're spreading our faith, which is the purest yet known to man. My Papa says Christianity is the religion of love."

"Yes, you've built canals," Ali said, "but you charge the peasants high fees to use the canal water for irrigation. Railroads need fuel and you're cutting down our forests to get it. You've also brought the opium trade. You tax the people without pity. And since they're too beaten down to rebel, you give yourselves credit for keeping the peace."

Ali raised himself from his cushions. He had clearly given these matters a lot of thought. Black eyes shining, he continued, "As for Christianity being *the* religion of love, just listen to this poem."

He took the book from James.

"It was written by a *Mussulman* a hundred years ago. It will show you that *other* religions know something about love! I'll translate it as I go along."

Jane gazed at the ceiling and her face assumed a pained expression.

People always look like that when they're forced to listen to someone read aloud, Catherine thought. She had seen that look when she insisted on sharing her favorite passages with her sisters.

Ali chanted in reverent tones:

"Love and Law are struggling.
Law says: 'Go to the mosque and learn the rules.
If you obey them, you will be saved.'
Love says: 'Close your books and put them away.
The place of love is the highest heaven.'"

"But I have always heard that Islam is a vengeful religion, preaching holy war against unbelievers. It's not thought to be a religion of love at all," Elizabeth said in a puzzled tone.

"Vengeance against people who disagree with you is a strand in Islamic thought," James Keats said. "But then, it's a strand in Christian thought as well. Remember the crusades. They got very ugly indeed."

"How do you know so much about it?" Jane asked, gazing at James admiringly.

"Like many English people, I started out believing that

Christianity is the highest form of religion. But as I studied Hinduism and Islam, I realized that all religions have both an angry side and a loving side."

"I think that *all* religions offer a path to God. But I wouldn't tell that to Reverend Brown. He'd denounce me from the pulpit if I did," Catherine said.

"I believe in God," James said, "but I don't believe in any particular religion's version of god. I think that any one can find God who really *wants* to find Him."

Elizabeth shook her head. "You're all talking about the best way to find God, but I don't think God even exists," she blurted out suddenly.

A stunned silence followed. Elizabeth had often wanted to say what she'd just said, but she'd never dared to. No one she knew *ever* questioned the existence of some sort of God—or gods. And now she felt she had gone too far. James Keats's daring claim that all religions are equal had encouraged her to speak out. But even James had been shocked by her remark.

Ali tactfully changed the subject.

"As soon as I recover from my fever, James and I are going to visit you. It's one of the few things I really *want* to do that will please my grandfather. Your mother is such a sweet-looking lady. I never saw my own mother, but I like to imagine that she was a sort of Indian version of yours."

"Does your grandfather still think there is going to be trouble?"

"Yes, he does, even though the English are now saying that the *chapatti* business was just superstitious foolishness that is sure to blow over."

"Well, we must hope for the best, and meanwhile, we shall look forward to your visit," Jane said in her best social manner, as she rose to leave. James Keats looked at her with rapture, as if he were hearing the song of angels.

When the sisters got back to Shivapur, they told Fanny what a wonderful time they'd had on their ride and thanked her for staying at home.

"*Someone* had to take care of poor Mama," Fanny said, in a self-denying tone. "But I'm not sure it was right to deceive her."

"Oh, piffle," said Elizabeth, absentmindedly. She was mentally planning her painting of the Malior Palace. Should it include human figures or would they spoil the symmetry? She couldn't quite decide.

CHAPTER SEVEN: A PICNIC

When Catherine said that she had invited Ali and James to visit them, Mrs. May wasn't sure what to do. She reminded herself that it was only charitable to suppose that Mr. Keats had taught his dusky pupil to behave as an English gentleman should. Perhaps Ali was even one of those *natural* gentlemen about whom one heard so much. And she had to admit that Mr. Keats was a nice fellow.

But then she remembered that Mr. Keats had no fortune. He was nothing but a servant in the household of a native. It wouldn't do for him to get serious about Jane. And it certainly wouldn't help Catherine's already dim marriage prospects if it got around that she had befriended an Indian.

No, Mrs. May didn't want Ali to enter her house! And she would be almost equally relieved if his tutor stayed home as well.

Mrs. May knew better than to make these thoughts public. She could imagine how angrily Catherine and Elizabeth would react. Jane wouldn't be pleased either.

But her daughters could read her feelings in the tight compression of her lips. So Catherine decided to put some pressure on her mother. Meeting Mr. Beaglehole by chance, she told him that Mrs. May was planning to be "not at home" whenever Ali called.

As she had expected, Mr. Beaglehole was alarmed. "My dear Miss May, this would be the *worst* possible time to offend the *Nawab* of Malior. Your mother must not snub his grandson upon any account. She must welcome him to your home as if he were your long lost brother! I shall visit her myself and explain matters."

It was not easy for Mr. Beaglehole to convince Mrs. May that the station's survival in case of a mutiny outweighed the possible damage to her daughters' chances of finding husbands. But Mr. Beaglehole's word was law in Shivapur. Mrs. May agreed to receive Ali, and receiving Ali meant receiving James Keats as well.

By late March, Ali and his tutor had visited the Mays several times.

Mrs. May did not think that any Indian could be the social equal of her daughters. Not even an aristocrat like Ali. But her prejudice diminished in the face of Ali's friendliness. After all, she reflected, the boy was not personally responsible for his unfortunate complexion. Then too, poor fellow, he was an orphan!

So Mrs. May agreed to invite Ali and Mr. Keats when the family decided to have a picnic. Of course, the Mays still needed to economize, but such a party was hardly more expensive than staying at home.

Gaily they carried their baskets of food and wine to a glade near Shivapur's *maidan*, a big open area on which some British officers were having an impromptu polo match. An enormous banyan tree shaded the spot where they spread their blankets. The rest of the area, covered with a kind of creeping grass known as *doob*, was unsheltered and looked very dry indeed. One could practically see steam rising from the earth. The hot weather was coming.

The young people played an exhilarating game of blind man's buff, in the course of which Mr. Keats caught Jane several times. Everyone realized that he was peeping under his blindfold. Whenever he seized her, Jane erupted into a positive waterspout of happy giggles.

"Children, children," Mrs. May cried, her voice not quite so kind as usual, "that is *quite* enough. You are all getting very hot. Mr. Keats and Ali are perspiring, and even you girls are in quite a glow. It doesn't do to run around in the Indian sun at midday."

"If Ali and James were horses, we'd say they were sweating. Because they really are soaking wet," Elizabeth said mischievously. "But that would be quite improper. So we say they're 'perspiring' instead. And though the word 'glow' sounds nice, it doesn't really describe how soggy I am right now."

"Can't one of you suggest a quieter game?"

"Ellen Barnfather told me about a new game the other day," Jane said helpfully. "You know how fat Ellen is. She doesn't like to move. So not surprisingly, it's a quiet game. "

Fanny gave a little moan. Jane was almost as unkind about Ellen Barnfather as she was about Susan Brown.

"The game is called 'Write Your Own Masterpiece.' You sit in a circle and one person begins a story. She breaks off at an exciting place, and the next person continues. You can get some very amusing results."

Catherine liked the idea of a game that involved storytelling. She asked Fanny to begin.

"I can't invent a story," Fanny said modestly, "but if it's all right, I will tell you one that I read in a book called *Improving Tales*."

Everyone agreed, though no one seemed enthusiastic.

"There was once a girl named Amy whose family had very little money. One of her classmates came to school wearing a lovely sapphire bracelet. Amy wished with all her might that she had a sapphire bracelet of her own. Later the same day, Amy's classmate drew a picture of their teacher, with a monstrous hump and the words 'Young ladies, my eye is upon you' coming out of his mouth in a balloon. All the girls laughed because the teacher really did say that a lot. Amy was more jealous than ever of her classmate. But then the teacher seized the slate with the drawing, and he punished Amy's classmate. And so Amy realized that bracelets are not nearly as important as —"

Here Fanny broke off, certain the next player would know that the words "good behavior" were needed to complete her sentence. But Elizabeth continued,

"Artistic talent. After all, Amy's classmate had made the girls laugh by her skill at drawing, and being punished by a pompous old teacher was a small price to pay for that. Amy decided that the moral of the story was *not* that she should be a good girl—but that she should take drawing lessons. Since her family couldn't pay for them, she decided to get the money herself. She joined a gang of *dacoits*, and sent them to her classmate's house. They crept in through a window and escaped with a lot of loot. Amy's share was —"

"Six silk dresses," Jane said. "Amy tried on a blue dress

with a ruffled skirt, and she looked perfectly lovely. At that very moment an invitation came for the Prince's ball. Amy jumped into a coach, but when she arrived at the palace, she found that—"

"The ball had been canceled," Ali went on, "because the Prince had joined a rebellion against the Queen. He rode off with a ragged collection of peasants to meet the Queen's army. The Queen's soldiers had the latest weapons, while the Prince's men had only swords. But they fought the Queen's big battalions with the passion of desperate men. Their swords whirled above their heads. And in the end, the Prince's ragged army—"

"Lost the battle," Catherine continued, though she knew this was not what Ali wanted her to say. "But then the Prince discovered that the pen is mightier than the sword. He composed an ode to his gallant soldiers. 'When can their glory fade? Oh, the wild charge they made,' he wrote, feeling quite inspired. He hoped his poem would influence future generations to resist the Queen, even though the cause was lost for the moment, and—"

"He was right. For his poem was very popular," James interrupted, with a sympathetic glance at Ali. "Yet the Prince never again went to war. Instead, he rescheduled his ball, and at the ball his tutor, Mr. Peets, met Amy for the first time. Overwhelmed by her beauty, Mr. Peets walked her into the conservatory and proposed. Amy was absolutely delighted, so—"

"Perhaps that is enough of this rigamarole," Mrs. May cried, though James had not paused. "I think Jane ought to help me unpack the lunch." She gestured wildly in the direction of her daughter.

"I tried to tell an uplifting tale," Fanny said with a sniff. "But the rest of you twisted it this way and that to suit your own purposes."

"Well, that's the point of the game, isn't it?" Elizabeth said. "And art always expresses the artist's own interests and personality, anyway. No matter what the subject matter seems to be."

Elizabeth could never resist a chance to disagree with Fanny.

"You stole the Prince's poem from Alfred Tennyson's 'Charge of the Light Brigade,' which is about the Crimean War," James accused Catherine.

"Yes, I did," Catherine admitted.

"Tennyson's poem fit into your part of the story quite well. But I don't like patriotic verse," James said. "It usually exalts war—and wars never solve anything."

The group consumed a delicious lunch of sliced mutton, roast chicken, cheese, pickles, and Indian sweets. The Mays belonged to the Shivapur mutton club, which raised and slaughtered sheep for the station families to share. The English loved mutton, because it reminded them of home. Mussulmen were allowed to eat it, so it could be served to Ali.

The day was growing hotter. Catherine suggested another quiet game. "Do you know 'Truth'?" she asked James.

"It isn't always easy to tell what is true and what is false," he replied seriously. "So much depends on the angle from which one looks at a thing, as the ancient Jain holy men used to say. A day that seems hot to an Englishman may seem comfortable to a peasant who is used to working in the sun."

"I see what you mean, but I wasn't asking you about Indian philosophy. Though I know you're interested in it. 'Truth' is the name of a game. It's utterly simple. Everyone promises to give an honest answer to whatever question the other players ask them."

Mrs. May scented danger. It was hardly ladylike to express one's true feelings on certain subjects — or perhaps on any subject. But if she told her daughters that she didn't want them to play 'Truth," it would sound as though she were recommending *un*truth. And she certainly couldn't do that. Ladies and gentlemen were supposed to be above telling lies or even fibs.

Mrs. May sighed. Raising daughters was very difficult. Everywhere one turned one encountered some sort of prohibition. She decided to let the game go on.

Elizabeth asked the first question. "Fanny, do you enjoy being selfless because it makes you feel superior to the rest of us?"

"Superior?" Fanny said in a tone of genuine surprise, "how could I possibly feel superior to someone as pretty as Jane or as talented as you and Catherine? If I didn't try to be helpful, no one would care for me at all."

Elizabeth was silenced. What a nasty game "Truth" was. She vowed never to play it again.

To mark her withdrawal from the game, Elizabeth took

out her sketchbook and a charcoal pencil. Soon she was deeply absorbed in drawing a portrait of her mother. She giggled as she captured the frantic expression Mama's face had worn when James, the 'blind man,' caught Jane for the fourth time in a row.

Next, it was Ali's turn to ask a question. "Who do you think is the prettiest lady here?" he asked James.

"Miss Jane, of course. There cannot be two opinions on that point."

Jane glanced up at James from under her long eyelashes.

"Which lady do you most like to talk to?" Fanny asked James. She was sure she knew what his answer would be.

"Catherine," he said instantly.

Everyone was startled, James himself no less than the others. Jane grimaced. Catherine couldn't help smiling. Mrs. May's thoughts veered off in an entirely new and highly satisfactory direction.

At that moment, three of the English officers who had been playing polo rode up to speak to the Mays. They exchanged glances when they noticed Ali.

In his usual polished manner, Lieutenant Palliser inquired after the ladies' health and remarked that it was a rather hot day. But the other two officers, Captain Jones and Lieutenant Stapleton, were less polite. They put their heads together and spoke only to one another. At first their mutterings were inaudible, but suddenly a few words rang out. "That black bastard... Eating with white women. I'd like to..." There could be no doubt that Captain Jones wanted to be overheard.

Flushed with anger, Mrs. May struggled to her feet and drew herself up to her full height. "I'm afraid we must be going, gentlemen," she said stiffly, "Ali, dear, would you mind carrying Miss Jane's parasol? Mr. Keats, can you take charge of the basket?"

The girls gazed admiringly at their mother. Sometimes her responses were completely unexpected. It wasn't totally ridiculous for Ali to wish he had a mother like theirs.

CHAPTER EIGHT: BAD NEWS

When the Mays got home, they found Komal in a state of agitation.

"News, *Memsahib*, news. Terrible happening at Barrackpur. *Sepoy* by name of Mangal Pande is waving loaded rifle at officers. He is telling other *sepoy* to join him and is calling them *banchut* when they do not. I must not say what that bad word is meaning. Then he is wounding two Englishmen and fighting with colonel and general."

Catherine felt a throb of fear, like the one she had experienced on the ride to Malior. Her fears were not calmed when Komal went on to say that Mangal Pande had been arrested. Might not his rebellion be the prelude to a general mutiny among the *sepoys* or even a peasants' revolt?

The Mays immediately set out for the Residency. Mr. Beaglehole would surely have received the latest information by telegraph. They found most of the Shivapur civilians gathered in the Residency drawing room. Mrs. Beaglehole was giving them strong tea and brandy. Mr. Beaglehole walked about the room, soothing his guests.

"My dear Mrs. May, do not agitate yourself unnecessarily. The incident with Pande took place yesterday. He has already been tried by a court martial and sentenced to be shot. To show other *sepoys* that the Company's rule is just, he was tried by a tribunal composed entirely of native soldiers. The sentence will be carried out shortly."

"Oh, Mr. Beaglehole, please excuse a lady's fear, but may I ask you, might not Pande's regiment mutiny to prevent his execution? Of course, I don't pretend to know as much as you do, but surely these *sepoys* hang together? My husband always says the younger English officers haven't tried to win their loyalty."

"Your husband is right about that, I'm afraid, but even so... don't try to second guess us *sahibs*, Mrs. May. We have studied the native mind and we have the situation under control. We have already disarmed and disbanded Pande's regiment. His mates did seem to be on the brink of rebellion, but now they've all been sent home. Our firm response should stop other regiments from rebelling."

Catherine had been listening closely.

"But Mr. Beaglehole, the *sepoys* in Mangal Pande's regiment *didn't* mutiny. Not actually. Yet you punished them anyway. Won't that frighten the other regiments too much? Other *sepoys* might decide that they shouldn't just wait around to be sent home. They might decide to attack us while they still have their rifles. Shouldn't we take precautions?"

"That is very ingenious, Miss May," Mr. Beaglehole said calmly, "but I fear it is quite wide of the mark. Please do not indulge your feminine imagination in this tricky situation. What we need now is an appearance of complete confidence. If Jack *Sepoy* perceives weakness or fear among us, he will attack like a shark smelling blood. No, you must return home and stay calm, like the sensible little girl you are."

Catherine was silenced.

"In this terrible plight," Mrs. Brown said, taking advantage of the pause, "I must testify for Jesus. These trials have been sent as punishment for our sins. We have been extravagant. We have prided ourselves on the beauty of our daughters, thinking nothing of their spiritual welfare. We have made friends with the godless heathen instead of trying to convert him."

Here she cast a very pointed glance in Mrs. May's direction.

"God is not mocked," she concluded.

"Amen," Reverend Brown added.

Elizabeth glared at the Browns. Fanny patted her mother's arm consolingly.

There was nothing to do but to go home and wait. As the Mays walked away from the Residency, the sky turned from brilliant blue to velvety black. There was no moon, but millions of stars glittered brightly. Gazing up at the Milky Way, the sisters felt calmer. But Mrs. May remained worried.

"It's been some time since we heard from your Papa. A letter should have come last week. How awful if there should be a mutiny while he is still in the countryside. We might well be separated for a long time... perhaps forever."

"Yes," said Elizabeth, "I think the situation is a lot worse than old Beaglepoop says. He knows it, too. And if the worst happens, it's going to be hard on Ali as well as on us. His grandfather will side with the English, but Ali's sympathies will be with the rebels."

"I wonder what James would do if there were a

mutiny," Catherine said. "He isn't exactly your typical *pukka sahbib*. His beliefs are nothing like the Browns' or even like Papa's. He has studied Indian thought so much that he's become a sort of white native. He doesn't admire the Company's *raj* at all."

"That's true," Elizabeth agreed. "Ali isn't a black Englishman to nearly the same degree, even though his grandfather has tried to turn him into one."

"Yes, it will be difficult for James," Jane said softly.

"Actually," Elizabeth said, "it's going to be more difficult for many Indians than for James. In the end he will certainly support the English. But what about Komal? She is very fond of us, and we love her too. She won't know what to do! Other natives will also face a dreadful conflict of loyalties."

"Yes," Fanny added, "and even if they resolve to act selflessly, as of course they should, that's not going to tell them what they ought to do, is it?"

"How nice to hear you admit that self-sacrifice isn't the solution to every imaginable problem," Elizabeth said tartly.

No sooner had the Mays entered the bungalow than Inder stepped forward holding a lamp. He handed Mrs. May one of the new telegraphic messages.

Mrs. May's fingers trembled as she opened it. The stuffed jackal on the table beside her, its lips drawn back in a permanent snarl, glared maliciously. The dark shadows in the hall closed in on her. She sank helplessly into the nearest chair. Elizabeth snatched the telegram from her hands: "Your husband very ill.

Cannot be moved. Come at once."

"How could they send a telegraphic message?" Jane asked. "Papa is miles away from the nearest town."

Elizabeth examined the envelope. "It was sent from Meerut. The station there has a telegraph office. Probably Papa's assistant went to Meerut with the message."

Some color returned to Mrs. May's face.

"Children," she said firmly, "I must go. I will borrow a carriage from one of our neighbors. *Not* the Browns, I think. Inder will go with me."

"But what about the unrest? Mangal Pande and all that. Won't you be in terrible danger if there is a rebellion?" Fanny said. She was on the verge of tears.

"I must go," Mrs. May repeated. "Your father has been my husband for almost twenty years. I can't leave him to die alone. Even if he *is* in debt. Inder will protect me, and you girls should be safe here at the station. Komal will look after you."

The sisters remained silent, and Mrs. May continued, "We must get ready. I shall leave tomorrow at first light. I must write to the Barnfathers to ask for their *palki-garry* and a horse to pull it. Komal, you will take the chit to their bungalow. Jane, pack some everyday clothes in my old valise. Catherine, collect wine and jellies from the storeroom. And anything else an invalid might want to eat. Arrowroot, perhaps. Elizabeth, get the medicine chest. It is under the bed in the guestroom. Fanny, you stay with me. I'll need someone to send if I think of anything else."

The sisters were amazed by their mother's efficiency. It seemed as if she had been waiting all her life for a real opportunity to use her wits. And now she was rising to the occasion. They scattered to obey her orders.

Underneath their sorrow, there ran an undercurrent of excitement. They would be left in charge of the house. The station was in danger. The routine of their Anglo-Indian life was breaking up.

None of the Mays got much sleep that night. Shortly after dawn, the family gathered in the hall. The Barnfathers' *palki-garry* was packed and Inder sat on the box in a white uniform and multi-layered turban, holding the reins. Mrs. May kissed her daughters.

She considered telling them that they were not to receive visits from *any* gentlemen until she returned. But she couldn't quite bring herself to do it. An occasional visit from Ali and Mr. Keats would certainly cheer the girls up. And they might well need cheering. Then too, Lieutenant Palliser, who had quite a large fortune, might call to see Jane if he heard that her father was ill. Perhaps the danger to their reputations was not all that important. Unusual times demand unusual measures.

Fanny sobbed as the carriage drove off. Catherine embraced her affectionately.

CHAPTER NINE: COPING

Mangal Pande went to the gallows. A battalion of British soldiers stood by in case of trouble — but nothing happened. A few days later, however, native regiments started showing signs of sullenness. Whenever they did, their English officers disarmed the men. This strategy of pre-emptive strikes seemed to be working. Catherine no longer questioned its wisdom. Elizabeth made no more remarks about "Beaglepoop's" stupid optimism.

As the first weeks of April passed and the weather grew hotter, the sisters' lives settled down. Jane took over her mother's housekeeping duties. Komal did Inder's work as well as her own.

As soon as her mother left Shivapur, Jane established her new routine. She went to the storeroom right after *chota hazri*, while the air still held a hint of coolness. The room was plain and practical. Rough wooden shelves held the rows of earthenware pots in which cooked food was stored. Big tins filled with staples covered a table whose legs stood in saucers of liquid paraffin.

The saucers were there to protect the tins from the insects that swarmed over the storeroom floor. Black ants, white ants, roaches, centipedes, crickets, and even an occasional scorpion drowned in the paraffin as they tried to climb up the legs of the table. This slaughter was absolutely necessary, for given the chance, the bugs would gobble candles and soap, as well as tastier things like flour and sugar.

Next, Jane and Komal decided on the menus for the day. The cook joined them and Jane weighed out the supplies that he would need. When he returned to the kitchen to grind spices in his mortar, Jane checked over her stocks of semolina, sago, and chutney to see what had to be bought at the bazaar.

Then Komal went off to do the marketing. A few *memsahibs* did this themselves, but Komal had convinced Mrs. May that she would get much better prices than any European possibly could. Not only did Komal have finely developed bargaining skills, but the vendors would never even *try* to cheat an Indian as they would a foreigner.

While Komal was at the market, Jane went out to the veranda to give directions to the *durzi*, who sat there cross-legged, sewing or mending. Then she opened her lacy parasol and headed for the garden. She told the *mali* which flowers to cut and which beds to weed. As Jane talked to him, she noticed that the violets and phlox were wilting in the broiling sun. If only her mother would stop trying to grow English flowers in this unsuitable climate.

Jane's work for the day was now finished, although she would have to check up on the servants occasionally to make sure they were not slacking off. It was barely ten o'clock.

Jane wondered why her mother's advice books talked about the *memsahib*'s work the way they did. *The Good Wife's Bungalow* made housekeeping in India sound like a terrifically demanding and important job. The book claimed that a woman could prove the superiority of the English race by managing her household efficiently. What a lot of nonsense! And the book told women to treat disobedient servants as harshly as the officers were treating the *sepoys*. Could that really be right? Jane had never doubted that British rule was good for India, but now she wasn't so sure.

Jane pushed these uncomfortable thoughts away. She loved her life in Shivapur, and she wanted to go on enjoying it. There is no sense in being too critical, she told herself. As the hour for receiving male callers approached, she went to her room to change her dress. How should she fix her hair? A chignon was very becoming, but a puffy pompadour might be even nicer...

After Mrs. May's departure, Catherine decided to stop the lessons she usually gave the younger girls. She felt that she was too utterly worried about her father to go on teaching. She needed to distract herself. She started writing a story about a handsome Englishman who was studying Indian philosophy at Oxford. He fell madly in love with an intelligent girl, rather like Jane Eyre, only much, much taller.

Elizabeth put her schoolbooks away and started her painting of the audience hall at Malior Palace. The beautiful room lived in her memory. She had only to close her eyes to see its every detail. As always when she painted or drew, she felt a rush of happiness. She mixed her colors carefully, forgetting all about her mother's absence and her father's danger.

Fanny went on with her lessons as usual. She missed Catherine's help, but of course she did not complain.

Poor Catherine was so worried about dear Papa that it wouldn't be right to make *any* demands on her. Fanny thought that if Mama and Papa ever found out how she had behaved in this emergency, they would surely approve. They might even praise her for bearing her burdens without troubling her sisters.

During these weeks, Lieutenant Palliser visited often, as also did James Keats. Since it would not be proper for Jane to receive male callers alone, Catherine remained in the drawing room during their visits.

James sometimes gazed at Jane with a mooncalf look, but he usually talked to Catherine while Jane was occupied with her other suitor.

The lieutenant always brought a big bouquet of flowers and spent much time whispering softly in Jane's ear. He sent her off into gales of laughter with his imitations of a *sepoy* making a horrible face while loading an Enfield rifle with one of the ill-fated cartridges.

Catherine winced. She knew that Jane didn't really think the *sepoys'* anger was a laughing matter. But Jane would do almost anything to make herself agreeable to an attractive man. Mr. Keats seemed to be losing out in the battle for Jane's affections. Catherine couldn't help being pleased by that.

The sisters grew more anxious about their father as the days passed. April was almost over when the *chuprassi* finally brought a letter. Elizabeth tore open the envelope and read it aloud:

"My dearest daughters,

Your Papa's condition has been so grave that I have not

had a spare moment in which to write you, though I know how worried you must be. But now I am happy to say that he is much better, indeed he is out of danger. I found him suffering from typhoid fever, an illness that worsens until it comes to a crisis. Of course, there is no doctor here in the countryside, but nursing is one of the few things that I *do* understand. A good woman should always be ready to risk her health and even her life to care for her loved ones when they are ill. Remember that, girls.

As the crisis approached, Papa's fever rose. He became delirious and moaned in a broken voice. 'Oh, horrors, oh, look! Look at my little women! They are playing harps... All four of them... How terrible they look with those great wings on their shoulders.'

I had to listen to these ravings for days as I watched the poor man toss in pain. I assured him that you girls had by no means turned into angels — quite the contrary — but it did not seem to ease his mind. He grew weaker and weaker.

Just when I was expecting the worst, his fever broke. Drenched in perspiration, he fell into a sound sleep, and he awoke refreshed. With time, he will regain his strength.

Meanwhile you must all behave with the utmost propriety. Do not see too much of Ali if you can avoid it without hurting his feelings.

Jane and Catherine, do not accept *any* — I repeat, any — marriage proposals until I return. Reply that you are deeply honored, but cannot engage yourself without your Mama and Papa's consent. If more is needed, say that you esteem him and will be a sister to him—whoever he may be.

I must return to Papa now, so can write no more. Send an immediate answer by the *chuprassi*. I miss you all.

Your loving mother, Caroline May

p.s. There are only a few signs of unrest in this area."

Hoping no one would notice, Elizabeth blinked back tears. She didn't want to start crying like that soppy weakling Fanny.

"Well," she said briskly, "that's certainly a relief. Papa's delirious ravings were actually more reasonable than some of the things he says when he's in full possession of his senses. He didn't like it when he thought we had grown wings. Maybe *now* he'll stop trying to make us behave like angels."

Catherine wondered why on earth her mother found it necessary to caution her against accepting a marriage proposal. Did Mama really think James Keats was going to propose because he enjoyed chatting with her? If only he would! But it wasn't very likely.

Jane's thoughts were similarly occupied.

"It's true that I might receive a proposal from James or Lieutenant Palliser or *both*," she said in a full, satisfied tone, "but it's hard to see who would propose to Catherine before Mama returns. Of course, Catherine is far more attractive than Susan Brown. For one thing, her nose is the appropriate color. And she has a much better figure than Ellen Barnfather. But still..."

Her voice trailed off as she saw the annoyance in her

sister's eyes. She hadn't meant to hurt Catherine's feelings. She had even gone out of her way to praise her sister's looks. And she had stopped herself from saying that Catherine usually looked like a walking rag bag. But apparently Catherine expected even more than this...

Fanny buried her head in the sofa cushions.

To reassure their mother, the sisters wrote that they were doing well on their own. The *chuprassi* left to deliver their letter.

According to the etiquette of British India, men were to call on ladies only from eleven to two. Many men hated paying visits in the hottest part of the day, when all one wanted was to tear off one's clothes, flop into bed, and tell the *punkahwallah* to start flapping his fan. But customs are hard to change, and the calling hours remained as originally established.

The clock was just striking four when Ali dashed into the Mays' parlor. Through the window, the girls could see the groom on his small bay pony, holding the reins of Ali's thoroughbred black mare.

"I have come in... great hurry. I know it's the wrong time," Ali panted. "But I had to tell you... such awful news. You'll understand... how I feel. Grandfather doesn't think I should be upset."

"Oh, dear, what can the matter be *now*?" Fanny moaned. "Life seems to be just one disaster after another these days. I'm not sure I can bear much more."

"Well, you'll have to," Elizabeth snapped. She also felt

anxious as she waited for Ali to stop gasping, but she was determined not to show it.

"For the last few weeks the angriest *sepoys* have been saying that any solider who touches the Enfield rifles will be out-casted. There is nothing a Hindu fears more."

"Why is that?" Catherine said. "I should think a low caste Hindu would be happy to escape from the caste system altogether."

"Not at all. An out-caste is even lower than an untouchable. No one will have anything to do with him. Because of this threat, the commanding officer in Meerut has been wondering if he should back down and tell the *sepoys* that they don't have to use the new rifles."

"I gather he decided *not* to back down," Elizabeth interrupted. Ali's state of excitement was proof of that.

"That's right. Because a lot of English troops are stationed in Meerut, he decided to be tough. He thought the English soldiers could keep things under control. So he ordered the *sepoys* to use the rifles. How stupid to give such an order at this time! How could he expect it to be obeyed?"

"Was it?" Catherine asked breathlessly.

"Of course not, Catherine. Haven't you been listening?" Ali snapped. He had recovered his breath. "Eighty-five men refused to fire their guns, and they were *all* arrested. They are to be tried by a court martial. James has ridden to Meerut to get more news."

"All right, all right, maybe I was being utterly slow on

the uptake. But I get it now. It's a disaster. What do you think is going to happen?"

"My grandfather and I think the men will be punished in some horrible way. Grandfather says they deserve it. He says it will put an end to these rumblings of rebellion. But I think the men are martyrs. Punishing them because they stood up for their faith is horribly unjust."

"I see your point of course," Elizabeth said, "but if this injustice puts an end to the unrest, perhaps it isn't a bad thing. People do sometimes say that the end justifies the means."

"I'm not sure I agree with that, though my grandfather would. But I don't believe for a minute that punishing these *sepoys* will stop other *sepoys* from mutinying. It will just add fuel to the fire. That's the only thing I'm pleased about."

"Ali, for heaven's sake, don't be so bloodthirsty. You're upsetting Fanny," Catherine cried. "And, Fanny, you must try not to worry so much. A mutiny isn't going to harm civilians. It's just a quarrel between the men and their officers. We won't even be involved."

But Fanny did not look convinced.

CHAPTER TEN: THE MUTINY BEGINS

In Meerut, the eighty-five rebellious *sepoys* were tried for insubordination by a native court martial. They were convicted and sentenced to ten years of hard labor.

Under a broiling sun, the men were taken to the parade ground under guard. There a ceremony of humiliation took place. They were stripped of their uniforms, shackled, and dressed as convicts.

Some of the oldest *sepoys* wept. "I have eaten the bread of the Company," one of them cried out, "And I want to be true to my salt. But I cannot disobey Allah, the most high."

During this ceremony, English troops stood by to prevent trouble, just as they had when Mangal Pande was hanged. Once again everything went smoothly. Chained together, the eighty-five men were marched off to prison.

James Keats heard this news when he rode into Meerut on May 10th. Convinced that nothing more would happen, he decided to stay until the next day. He wanted to rest up for his ride back to Malior.

But during the night, native cavalrymen stationed in the Meerut cantonment stormed the prison to free the convicted *sepoys*. These cavalrymen were joined by *sepoys* from the Meerut infantry regiments. Only a few Indian soldiers stayed loyal to the Company. A full-scale mutiny had begun.

The rebel soldiers rushed through the civil lines, shouting angrily, "For the faith... kill the foreigners!"

They set fire to every bungalow they passed and murdered every English man, woman, or child they met. Taken by surprise, the Europeans put up little resistance. Screams of agony and fear filled the air. Mutilated bodies littered the streets.

But many English troops remained in the cantonment, and the rebel soldiers knew that if they stayed they would be outnumbered. As soon as the surviving English officers recovered from their surprise, they would surely counter-attack. So the rebels left Meerut and marched toward Delhi, where there were fewer English soldiers.

The eighty-year-old Mughal Emperor, Bahadur Shah Zafar the Second, lived in Delhi, in the huge palace known as the Red Fort, a virtual prisoner of the English. He was merely their puppet, an aged bird in a gilded cage. The *sepoys* thought the Emperor might welcome the chance to reclaim some real power for his dynasty. They hoped he would agree to lead their rebellion.

Every British station had its *dak* bungalow, kept for the use of travelers. Often it was set apart from the civil lines where the Europeans lived. James Keats was alone and dead asleep in the *dak* bungalow of Meerut when the mutiny broke out. Wakened by cries and howls, he stumbled to the window. As he peered into the moonlit night, he realized what was happening. Dim figures chased other dim figures. The blade of an uplifted sword glittered. Dark shapes lay on the ground.

If news of the mutiny spread over the telegraph lines, the *sepoys* would lose the element of surprise, and they wouldn't want that to happen. So James felt sure that the mutineers had already cut the wires connecting Meerut with other British stations. His first duty, he decided, was to carry the news to Shivapur. If he got there quickly, Mr. Beaglehole could take steps to defend the station against the rebels.

James crept along the wall of the *dak* bungalow, taking advantage of the cover it offered. He dashed across the open space separating the bungalow from its stables and saddled his horse with trembling hands. He thanked God that the bungalow was so far from the scene of the slaughter. He might be able to get away without being seen.

Soon he was galloping south toward Shivapur.

The surrounding fields were flooded with silver light. Glancing behind him, James realized with relief that no one was pursuing him. He could see masses of mutineers marching eastward on the Delhi road. Their figures grew smaller with every minute that passed.

Why were the native soldiers killing women and children? James wondered. Surely they knew that this would provoke savage reprisals? Perhaps they were trying to prove that their English rulers were just flesh and blood by the simple method of slaughtering them *en masse*? Or was it just bottled-up rage venting itself in pointless violence?

James thought of Jane May's kittenish softness and shivered with distress. But when he thought of Catherine, he almost smiled. He wouldn't want to be the *sepoy* who tangled with her.

James rode on. The moon set. Millions of stars twinkled cheerfully, indifferent to his suffering and his fear. As the sun rose on the morning of May 11th, he reached the Residency in Shivapur. Mr. Beaglehole already knew that telegraph communication with Meerut had been mysteriously interrupted. James told him why.

Mr. Beaglehole was not completely unprepared for this news. He had never really been sure that the Company was in control of the situation — though of course he had tried to calm the Shivapur womenfolk by claiming that there was no real danger. Women were such timid creatures. It was never quite safe to tell them the truth.

Mr. Beaglehole went to work immediately. He sent his trusted *khansama* to the cantonment to tell the officers that their men might mutiny. He sent the *chuprassi* to round up the English families and bring them to the Residency, the most solid building in the station. If only it were more solid. It was certainly not a fortress!

He asked James Keats to go back to Malior and beg the *Nawab* to send his army to aid the Shivapur garrison. Surely the *Nawab* would agree. But the Malior army was so badly armed. The Company had a rule that the troops of native rulers could not carry guns — only swords and *lathis*. These long bamboo staves tipped with brass, like the swords, could only be used at very close range. How unfortunate that was. Then, too, it would take the Malior army some time to arrive.

Mr. Beaglehole sighed heavily and went to review the Residency's defenses.

One by one, the station families gathered in the Residency drawing room.

Warned of the danger, the cantonment's commanding officer, Colonel Wentworth, ordered his *sepoys* to lay down their arms. He intended to send them home as soon as he got his hands on their guns. But the *sepoys* did not obey. Instead, they marched toward the Residency, waving their swords and old-fashioned 'Brown Bess' muskets. They had not yet been issued the new Enfield rifles.

The terrified civilians saw them approach through the drawing room windows. Fanny could not bear to look, but her sisters watched in horrified fascination.

There were no native cavalry stationed in Shivapur. The only horses in the cantonment belonged to English officers. Led by Colonel Wentworth, a group of English officers galloped into the civil lines only minutes behind the rebel infantrymen.

The officers overtook the *sepoys* just before the marching men reached the Residency. They rode through the crowd, slashing this way and that with razor sharp swords. Jane cried out as she saw Lieutenant Palliser behead a tall *sepoy* who had nearly dragged him from his horse. Looking almost like a cannonball, the man's dark head bounced once and then rolled slowly to a stop.

The mounted officers had opened up a small lead over the mutineers by the time they galloped into the Residency gardens. They leapt to the ground. Without tethering their horses, they rushed inside and locked the doors. But how was the Residency to be defended?

Colonel Wentworth moved into action. He stationed men with guns at all the windows. Other officers, armed only with swords, stood ready to rush out and attack should the rebels break down the doors. But the number of defenders was pitifully small. Waves of *sepoys* were running toward the Residency. They carried a log to use as a battering ram.

They were shouting the same slogans James had heard in Meerut, "For the faith, brothers. Do not weaken. Kill the foreigners."

A crowd of dirty, emaciated, half-naked natives collected behind the charging *sepoys*. They too were screaming insults.

"The English are made of uncooked dough," yelled a small man in a ragged *dhoti*. "They let their wives dance in public like *nautch* girls. They are few and we are many. Why should we fear them?"

As the *sepoys* approached, Colonel Wentworth gave the order to fire. Rifle shots rang out from the Residency's windows.

Many *sepoys* fell, but the surging waves did not retreat. Without even pausing, the attacking *sepoys* ran over the bodies of their comrades.

Although their old 'Brown Bess' muskets had a shorter range than the new Enfield rifles, the *sepoys* were soon close enough to fire at the Residency's windows with deadly effect. Bullets flew into the drawing room.

One of them struck Mrs. Brown, shattering her shoulder. Red blood soaked her sleeve. Reverend Brown knelt near her, praying loudly. Her screams were terrifying. Susan Brown stood by sobbing.

Jane stared numbly at Susan's nose. She couldn't

remember why she had ever been interested in it.

The other May girls had taken cover behind a sofa. Fanny cowered in Catherine's arms. But suddenly, she jumped to her feet.

"Papa, Papa," she cried hysterically, "they will burn the bungalow. Papa's papers will be destroyed. Papa will never survive the blow. I must save them, whatever the cost."

Catherine made a wild grab at Fanny's skirts, but her sister slipped past her and rushed out the Residency's back door. Her sisters realized that Fanny was headed for their bungalow to rescue the papers. Jane and Catherine chased after her.

Elizabeth wondered if it would be worth risking her life to save Fanny, but in the end she went too. She wasn't about to let herself be separated from Jane and Catherine.

As Elizabeth sprinted outside, the heat struck her like a blast from a furnace. Terrified, she gritted her teeth. Their bungalow was at the opposite end of the civil lines, and it surely would not be safe to take the direct route down the main avenue. She would have to thread her way through a tangled maze of back lanes in the native quarter. She hoped her sisters had done the same.

To her surprise, Elizabeth met no one on the way. A strange peace reigned in the alleyways behind the civil lines.

The richer Indian citizens of Shivapur were mostly cowering in their shops and homes, while many of the poorer ones had joined in the siege of the Residency. The mutiny was turning into a rebellion.

And the rebellion was already starting to look like a war between rich and poor. Most of the Indians who owned property were afraid of change, so they sided with their English rulers. But many ordinary Indians, who had absolutely nothing to lose, joined the rebel *sepoys*.

Fanny reached home only a few moments before her sisters. Komal held the door open for the girls and swiftly closed it behind them.

The new *dhobi*, Devender, was in the hall. Incredibly, he had just delivered a large load of freshly washed and neatly folded clothes. His old mare and empty four-wheeled cart stood in the shade of a big neem tree.

Fanny rushed into her father's study and emerged with two boxes of papers. She looked triumphant and just a bit mad.

The other girls gradually stopped panting. They weren't sure what to do next.

Komal took charge.

"There is much danger, my daughters," she said. "Anything can be happening at Residency. Too many *sepoys*. Must not be returning there. Let us be watching."

Komal went into the dining room, whose windows commanded a view down the wide, straight avenue that ran the length of the civil lines. The Residency stood at its head. She was peering out the window when Devender and the girls joined her.

The attackers had reached the door of the Residency and were trying to batter it down. Again and again, they slammed into it. Suddenly it gave way.

English officers rushed out through the breech. The front lawn of the Residency became the scene of a desperate hand-to-hand battle. The officers were good fighters. But so were the *sepoys*. They began to overpower their outnumbered opponents.

It was not long until there were only a few Englishmen left standing. They retreated into the Residency, pursued by screaming *sepoys*. The ragged mob did not follow. Perhaps they were still in awe of everything the Residency had symbolized for so many years.

The sisters had no idea what was happening inside the Residency. And they were too far away to hear anything but a formless roar, punctuated by shrieks. Gradually, the noise died down. One by one, *sepoys* began to leave the Residency. But no English men, women, or children were to be seen.

The May girls clutched Komal. They needed an adult to turn to.

"Oh, Komal!" Jane cried. "Surely they cannot *all* be dead?"

"I am not knowing," the *ayah* said. "Maybe some are escaping by back door. Maybe some are running into jungle. Maybe. Cannot know."

Elizabeth returned to the window.

"Oh, God," she screamed, "the Residency is burning. Is there nothing we can do?"

Catherine joined her. She looked out at the black smoke rising from the building that, more than any other in Shivapur, represented the past, stability, and safety.

"We must save ourselves," she said slowly.

CHAPTER ELEVEN: THE ESCAPE

Only Komal and Devender remained. The other servants had fled.

The girls knew why Komal was staying with them. She loved them like a mother. But why was Devender staying? He was only a *dhobi*, recently hired. If the rebels found him helping an English family, they would certainly kill him.

Komal answered their unspoken question.

"Devender is old friend. That is why I am making him *dhobi* when other *dhobi* go off. Very good man. Very smart. He is not leaving me. He knows I am not leaving you. But what to do? I must be thinking."

It was clear to Komal that the sisters must flee. The *sepoys* were slaughtering English women and children. If they found the girls when they came to burn the bungalow, they would kill them. And they would probably kill her and Devender as well. If the rebels caught them trying to leave Shivapur, the result would be the same. The girls might try disguising themselves, but Jane's big blue eyes and golden hair would surely give them away. There was no way that Fanny could pass for an Indian either. Komal gazed at the girls in despair.

Even Elizabeth felt paralyzed. She almost wished she had stayed at the Residency. If she had, she'd be dead, and her sufferings would be over. No, no, that was stupid. She must get a grip on herself. While they were alive and together, there was still some hope.

Then Komal came up with a plan. She began to issue

orders.

"Children, go to bedrooms. You must be taking off petticoat, taking off drawers, taking off corset. Putting on heaviest shoe. Plain dress. No ruffle. I go for food and water. Fanny, put papers down. Cannot be taking them."

Fanny clutched her father's papers for a few long moments, then dropped them with a cry. She heard the authority in Komal's voice.

Jane ran to her bedroom. She didn't own any really heavy shoes, but at least she had a flat-heeled pair. She slipped out of her pretty pink dress and stripped off one layer of underwear after another. She struggled into one of her shabbiest frocks. Without a corset, the bodice didn't fit right. Without her crinoline and hoops, the skirt seemed to cling to her legs. She must look disreputable. It was almost like going out naked.

Catherine changed her clothes with very different feelings. Without corset and petticoats, she felt light and strong. She put on the stout boots she had brought from England and thought that she would be able to walk many miles in them. It was utterly absurd to feel pleasure under these desperate circumstances. But nonetheless she did.

Soon everyone was back in the hall. Komal had brought tins filled with water, some bread, and a few pots of cooked food. Devender stood by. Unlike the May sisters, he did not look at all puzzled. He seemed to understand what Komal had in mind.

"Children," Komal said, "we must be going to my

home village. Very small village, called Murarmau. Village is very deep in jungle. Pushpa is there and she will be hiding us."

"But, Komal," Elizabeth said, "we will never be able to get there. We are sure to meet some of the mutineers on the way, and then..." Her voice trailed off miserably.

"Lizzie is right," Catherine cried. "It would be utterly insane to try to pass all the way through Shivapur. And we'd have to do that to get to the road. They'd see us and murder us. We're safer hiding here. Maybe English soldiers from Meerut will come in time to rescue us."

"But English solider maybe not coming. Or *sepoy* getting here first. Many *sepoy* coming up avenue now. I am seeing from window. We must go to Murarmau. Look at this," Komal said in a triumphant voice, and she held up a small pot filled with ashes and cinders. "I am taking from stove in kitchen."

The girls stared at her in amazement. How on earth could a pot of ashes help them to escape?

"We will be putting ashes on clean clothes Devender has brought. Then it will be looking like Devender is taking dirty things home for washing. Under clothes you are hiding. When cart far from Shivapur, we are leaving it. We will go to Pushpa."

"Won't that be very dangerous?" Fanny asked anxiously. She hated to challenge an adult, but she felt sure she'd die if she had to lie under a pile of laundry waiting to be hauled out and murdered.

"Yes. But is best way. Is only way. Cannot stay," Komal said firmly.

Fanny, as always, bowed to the voice of command. The other girls felt that Komal was right. They set about soiling the clean laundry that Devender had delivered. He helped them in silence.

Once again, Catherine felt an unexpected thrill of pleasure. Never had she been told to mess up her clothing *as a duty*. It had always been something that got her into trouble. She scattered cinders with a free hand.

Devender put the food and water in the back of his cart. Crouching low, the May sisters crept towards the cart. They climbed in and lay down next to the jars and tins, trying to make themselves as small as possible. Devender and Komal covered them with a huge pile of laundry.

Fanny told herself that the clothing wasn't dirty with bodily secretions. It was just clean laundry on which the ashes from a *sanitary* charcoal fire had been sprinkled. Nonetheless, she shuddered with disgust as she fought off panic. The cart lurched forward.

Time passed so slowly that it seemed to have come to a stop. The girls were hardly able to breathe under the heavy pile of clothing. The heat was intense. Sweat ran into their eyes.

"I wonder whether Mama would say I'm 'glowing' if she saw me now," Elizabeth thought. But she forgot about her mother as she grew thirstier. She would do anything for a glass of cold water. Or even warm water.

The cart suddenly stopped and rough male voices spoke to Komal and Devender in Hindi. Under all that laundry, it was impossible for the girls to hear anything clearly. But they realized that Devender must be acting the part of an unusually stupid *dhobi*. Stupid enough to go about his business in the middle of chaos.

His act could not have been completely successful, for suddenly a bayonet blade was thrust through the pile of clothes. It stuck fast in the floor of the cart, missing Jane by inches. Seconds later, someone wrenched it out.

Jane felt sure that the next thrust would strike her. A scream rose in her throat, but she gritted her teeth and forced it back. She would not betray them. Even if the blade slashed her face, she would remain silent. But no second thrust came. The owner of the bayonet had apparently decided that no one was hidden under the laundry. Jane clutched her nose and wept silently with relief.

The cart moved again.

Gradually the sounds of Shivapur receded. The sisters realized that the immediate danger was over. They must have reached the countryside by now.

The jolting of the cart increased. The girls clutched at the rough boards beneath them as they were shaken from side to side. Catherine thought that they had probably left the road and were bumping over a field.

"Oh, what are we going to do? Oh, what will become of us now?" Fanny murmured in time to the rocking of the cart. The soft chanting seemed to calm her.

Suddenly, the cart came to a halt. The sisters felt the laundry being pushed aside.

"Quick, girls. We are leaving cart. Now."

Catherine straightened her stiffened body. One of her feet had fallen asleep. She managed to crawl to the edge of the cart and drop to the ground. She stood there hopping on her good leg. Her sisters followed.

They were standing at the very edge of a jungle. On one side of them, under a hot sun, stretched golden fields of mustard. On the other, in deep shade, tangles of thick foliage blocked the view. You really can't see this forest for the trees, Catherine told herself. It amused her that the proverb had a literal meaning, as well as a figurative one.

"Into jungle. Carrying jars. Now," Komal commanded, handing them the supplies.

Without a word, Devender turned the cart around and plodded back across the fields towards the road. No one else was in sight.

The sisters plunged into the dark jungle. They knew that they were safer there than in the open, but all the same, they were frightened. Komal fought her way forward, through masses of creepers that seemed to reach out to grab her. She held back the thorniest branches so the girls could follow.

Birdsong and the hum of insects filled the air. Everything was intensely alive, intensely green, intensely threatening.

Jane stumbled over a root and cried out in pain. Her dainty slippers were far too thin for this sort of walking. If you could call it walking. It was more like threading one's way through an obstacle course. And it was incredibly hot. She felt like a vegetable in a steamer. Jane was so uncomfortable that she almost forgot her fear.

Fanny kept glancing back over her shoulder. The bodice of her old frock was drenched in sweat. Soon, she felt too tired and faint to take another step. She had eaten nothing that day. But she must not slow the others down. She trudged on.

They fought their way through the jungle for hours, covering very little ground. It was late afternoon when they reached a spot where the trees and vines were not so dense. It could almost be called an open glade. Sprays of purple orchids twined about the branches of the nutmeg trees that fringed the clearing. They sank to the ground, exhausted.

Komal opened one of the tins of water. She warned them to drink sparingly. The water would have to last for days. Elizabeth couldn't help swallowing more than her share. But Fanny made up for it by taking *less* than hers.

Catherine walked to the edge of the clearing and climbed onto a log. She peered into the jungle. It seemed impenetrable. Yet they had penetrated it. Again, Catherine felt that sensation of lightness and freedom. What infinite possibilities for change a single life could hold! She wondered what she would be doing a month from now. *If* she lived.

Suddenly, the log on which Catherine was standing shifted. She jumped back in alarm. The log slowly writhed and slithered off into the underbrush. Good Heavens! How utterly exciting. She had actually been standing on a huge python. She wished she could tell

James. He was always saying that the English should try to learn more about the real India. Standing on a python was a *very* real experience.

Komal took out some of the bread they had brought. The sisters were starving. As they wolfed down the food, Komal cleared her throat. She looked embarrassed. She seemed to be forcing herself to speak.

"Girls, listen. When I am becoming your *ayah* so many years ago, I am speaking no English. So your mama is telling me I can speak Hindi to you children. When Catherine is eight, your mama is wanting to send her to school in England. By then I am talking English. But I do not talk good English, because I know that your mama is not wanting me to do that."

"Really? Why not?" Catherine asked.

"If I talk good English, I am not sounding like servant. I am sounding like *memsahib*. Your mama is not liking this. But even more she is not liking daughters to talk Hindi any longer."

"Really? Why not?" Catherine repeated.

"She is saying daughters pick up bad Indian ways from talking Indian language. She is saying Catherine must be talking like English girl or they will not be liking her in England. So she is telling me not to talk Hindi to you any more. Always English. And always bad English. Of course, I am doing what she tells me. I am having no choice."

"I remember when you stopped talking Hindi to us," Catherine said suddenly. "And that's when Mama told *us* that we were never to speak Hindi again. I think we all spoke it quite well at that time, even Fanny, young as she was. But of course we obeyed Mama too."

"Yes," said Jane, "and most of the other servants spoke a bit of English as well. They would try to talk it to us. So we really never used our Hindi again."

"Have you forgotten?" Komal asked in Hindi.

The sisters shook their heads. Of course they hadn't forgotten. They had never stopped understanding the language. They always knew what the servants were saying when they talked to one another. But they had pretended to forget so as not to upset their mother. Apparently they had fooled Komal as well.

"It is a blessing that you can still understand," Komal continued in Hindi. "For when we get to my village, only Pushpa and her father will speak English. If you are to live in Murarmau, you will have to talk with the villagers. And you must talk to them in Hindi. Should mutineers come looking for foreigners in the village, it will help that you speak our language. Elizabeth and Catherine have dark eyes and hair. If they speak Hindi, they can pass for Indians."

"Good," Catherine said in Hindi. "From now on we speaks English only to each other. If we speaks to Komal or other Indians, speak only Hindi."

Komal was amused that Catherine's Hindi was far more halting than her own English. In that language, the tables were turned and it was Catherine who sounded like an uneducated servant.

But Komal was pleased that Catherine could still speak some Hindi. The other girls had spent their whole lives in India and probably remembered much more than Catherine did. Certainly, all the girls would quickly improve with practice. And that might well increase their chances of survival.

Catherine reached inside her dress and pulled out a small notebook.

"Ouch. This has been poking me in the side unmercifully. I have a pencil in here too, somewhere."

"Why did you hide them?" Fanny asked in a faintly reproachful tone. Keeping secrets was almost deceitful. People should never do anything they had to conceal.

"Oh, I can't live without writing, and there's going to be a lot to write about now. I feel certain of that. I shall use the notebook as a diary. But if I'd told you I was bringing a notebook, Lizzie would have insisted on bringing her paints and sketchbook, which are *much* bulkier. So I thought I'd avoid the issue."

"Well, I like that!" Elizabeth said. "There'll be just as much to paint as to write about! I wish I'd thought to bring my paints, but it never occurred to me. I was too scared to think clearly."

"Tell yourself that you left your paints behind to lighten our load, Lizzie," Catherine said with a smile. "Pretend it was intentional. Then you can see what it feels like to be selfless. Maybe you'll come to enjoy it, as you say Fanny does."

Elizabeth grimaced with annoyance. Fanny couldn't help smiling.

Somewhat rested, the group trudged on. Komal feared they might be lost. She had a pretty good idea of the direction they had to take, but it was so easy to get confused in a jungle. There was only the setting sun, gleaming through the thick foliage, to tell her which way they were going. Unless they found the path she was looking for, they might wander about until they died of thirst.

But their luck held. Just as Komal was about to despair, she gave a sudden, surprising cry of joy.

"Yes, here it is," she said in Hindi, "the path I was looking for. The men from Murarmau use it when they come out to hunt wild pigs during the cold weather. It leads straight from the village to the hunting grounds, so no other villages use it. On this path, we will not be seen, and better still, we will not get lost."

Fanny was not pleased to hear that there were wild boars in the area. It occurred to her that where there were tasty pigs, there might also be tigers, jackals, and leopards. She thought she heard a muffled grunt, but decided not to tell the others. They were braver than she was. It might not occur to them to worry until they actually spotted a boar or a tiger. She didn't want to frighten them needlessly. But why was she always left to suffer alone?

At sunset, they reached another open glade, where they decided to stop for the night. They drank tepid water and ate curried chicken with their fingers. Jane couldn't stop herself from using a little of the precious water to wash her hands.

Two of the pots were now empty and could be left behind the next day. Fanny was glad of that. At her own insistence, she had been carrying more than her share of the supplies.

The sisters lay down on the bare ground, after clearing away as much brush as they could. Mosquitoes immediately attacked. Elizabeth tried covering her head with her long skirt, but then they bit her legs. When she pulled the skirt down again, they swarmed around her face. By this time, she was too tired to care. She fell asleep.

For the next three days, they marched steadily along the path.

Jane's slippers disintegrated. She bound her feet with strips of cloth torn from Komal's *sari* and walked on as best she could. Lieutenant Palliser would be heartbroken if he knew what was happening to her. But he might be dead. And even if he were still alive, he might well be taking care of Susan Brown or Ellen Barnfather. In either case he wasn't available to pity her. A tear rolled down her cheek.

Food and water were in short supply, but Komal said there was enough to get them to the village. They would just have to ration what was left.

Catherine was amazed that they met no predators, animal *or* human. She almost wished that they could have one more adventure before they reached the village. Almost, but not quite.

On the third day, without warning, Elizabeth dropped down in the middle of the path. "I can't go a step further," she said in English, "I'm covered with bug bites. I'm as dirty as a sweeper. I'm weak and dizzy. Just leave me here to die, will you?"

She burst into tears.

"Elizabeth," Fanny said solemnly before Komal could speak, "it is extremely childish of you to give way like this. I thought you were supposed to be the strong one. The self-reliant one. The rest of us are also suffering. Think of *Pilgrim's Progress* and bear your own burdens. We're certainly not going to leave you here to die, and we can't carry you."

Elizabeth glared at Fanny, but did not rise. Fanny blushed at her own boldness.

Suddenly, a long, silver cobra slithered onto the path, close to where Elizabeth was sitting in a crumpled heap. The snake reared its hooded head and hissed angrily. Its sinister black eyes looked straight at her. She could see its forked tongue flickering in and out, out and in. Mesmerized, she froze in fear. But after a long minute, the cobra lowered its hood and retreated. As soon as it disappeared in the underbrush, Elizabeth jumped to her feet and walked on, more quickly than she had done in days.

That afternoon, the village of Murarmau appeared in the distance. Komal said they would be there in an hour. To celebrate, they drank the remaining water. Nothing had ever tasted quite so good.

CHAPTER TWELVE: THE VILLAGE

As Catherine limped into the village, she was appalled. Shacks with walls of gray mud leaned against each other, looking as if one good rainstorm would melt them. In the open bazaar, there were a few rickety stalls. They were selling only basic necessities, like lentils and millet.

Between the houses ran a complicated web of dirt paths, worn by the feet of villagers as they went about their daily tasks. A bullock cart was passing slowly along one of these paths, raising a cloud of stinging dust. A spotted dog lay sleeping in the middle of another path, his lean sides moving visibly as he breathed. A scorching wind seared the earth.

Some women were gathered at the *ghat*, the bathing steps that descended the bank of a small river, gossiping and dipping up clay pots of water. The water was green with algae, but it still looked cool and inviting. Small, naked children sitting on the lowest step dabbled their feet in the river. Catherine wished she could plunge in. Salty sweat covered her body. For the first time in her life, she felt dirtier than she wanted to be. Would wonders never cease?

Slightly separated from the rest of the village stood a large brick house. It was the only building of two stories in Murarmau, and it had a wooden roof, glass windows, and a stone patio. The doorways were surrounded by glazed tiles with a handsome floral pattern in shades of pink and green. By comparison to the rest of this impoverished place, it seemed luxurious. Even in absolute terms, Catherine thought it looked pretty comfortable.

Some of the fields surrounding the shacks and the bazaar were nothing but bare, ploughed earth. Others were planted with crops that looked nearly ripe. Little patches of lovely golden wheat and gray-green barley bowed before the wind. Catherine had seen these grains growing in England, where all grain was referred to as "corn." But in other small plots, wheat or barley was mixed with a plant that Catherine couldn't identify. Did these backward farmers think their crops would thrive without being weeded? No wonder everyone looked so poor.

The dark, tangled forest through which they had walked for so many days pressed against the edges of the planted fields. It looked as if it were waiting to retake the village.

To Catherine's relief, Komal headed straight for the substantial house, which must surely be the home of Pushpa's father, Ramu Ghosh, the village *zamindar*. With luck, they could all live there while they waited for the British to restore order.

Eager as she was for adventure, Catherine did not fancy an extended stay in a one-room mud hut. She couldn't begin to imagine how she would turn a dreary experience like *that* into fiction.

Without knocking, Komal walked through the door of the brick house. Slowly and shyly, the sisters followed her into a sitting room furnished with a divan and a European table and chairs. An altar with an elephant-headed *Ganesh* and other strange deities stood in a corner. Shafts of bright light from the open windows fell on the polished wooden floor.

Pushpa and Mahendra were sitting at the table, bent over a small book, their heads just touching. A reading lesson was in progress.

An older man in a neat *dhoti* and a spotless tunic was looking on. His golden skin and general resemblance to Pushpa proclaimed him her father.

As her cousin entered, Pushpa jumped to her feet.

"Komal! You're alive! Thanks be to Durga!" she cried in Hindi. "News of the mutiny came to us last week, but no one could tell us anything about Shivapur—they didn't even know if anyone who worked for the English escaped. We thought you had probably been killed."

Komal explained how Devender had helped them to flee.

"Devender may be only a *dhobi*," Pushpa said, smiling at Komal, "but he can be counted on in a crisis."

Pushpa's expression hardened as she noticed the four disheveled May girls, who now stood silently behind their *ayah*.

"Komal!" she said again, and this time her voice sounded angry. "How could you bring them here? Are you mad? You know all about the peasants' rumor mill. The English call it the 'jungle telegraph' because it sends news around so quickly. If these girls stay in Murarmau, the rebels will soon hear about it. Then who knows what they'll do to us? No, the girls can't possibly stay."

"But there is no place else for them to go," Komal said in a shaky voice. "They are almost like daughters to me. How can I let them die without trying to save them?"

"Oh, Komal, you're a soft-hearted fool. They're the children of a Company official. How do you think they will act when they're grown up? Just like the other *memsahibs*! They will say that Indian women are not pure. They will say that every Indian man wants to rape them."

"Oh, no," Komal protested, "they would never do that."

"Oh, wouldn't they? Don't be silly, Komal. These girls are trouble. For all you know, an Englishman may some day desert his Indian wife to marry one of them! They may be 'like daughters' to you, but Mahin really is a son to me. I won't have him put in danger for the sake of foreign devils. They must leave right now. If you love them so much, you can go with them. If not, send them alone!"

There was a silence. This was the last thing the sisters had expected. All of them had thought that if they could just reach Pushpa, they would be safe. That she would be as loyal to them as Komal was.

Komal could think of nothing more to say. After all, her reasons for wanting to rescue the girls were purely personal. Pushpa was right about that. And how could she argue that her love for them should outweigh Pushpa's love for Mahendra? It was true that they might cause terrible trouble for the villagers, Mahin included. She hadn't thought about that because she was so desperate to save them.

"You can't send us back to that awful forest," Elizabeth suddenly cried out. "What a horrible person you are! No matter what you do, I won't go. I couldn't stand it."

Remembering the heat, the thirst, and the hissing cobra, she dropped her face into her hands. She felt thoroughly humiliated by own weakness, but she was unable to fight it.

Pushpa looked at Elizabeth with contempt. *"Why should Mahin..."* she began angrily, when her father interrupted her.

"Pushpa, dear," Mr. Ghosh said in authoritative tones, "I took you in when you came home as a refugee. I lied to the villagers about your marriage so that they would not out-caste you for eating the foreigner's food and sharing his bed."

"Of course you did," Pushpa snapped. "Mahin and I are your own flesh and blood."

"No, I didn't do it only because you are my daughter. I also did it because you are a human being. We owe every living being protection against cruelty and evil. I do not have to tell you that murder is an evil. We may well be able to protect these girls, and we must try to do so."

"Isn't it enough that you are giving away Mahin's inheritance?" Pushpa cried. "Must you give away his life as well?"

"What will Mahendra think if we send these girls to die in the forest of hunger and thirst? What kind of Hindu will he become if he sees us ignore what human decency demands? You would see this yourself if your own experiences had not been so bitter. No, daughter, I know that I am right about this."

Pushpa did not look convinced, but she answered submissively. Clearly she was used to deferring to her father.

"Father, you have spoken indeed. I hope you will not regret it. If we are to hide these foreigners, we must decide quickly what is the safest way to do so. Safest for us as well as for them."

Pushpa said nothing more about her son's inheritance, and Catherine wondered why she had accused Mr. Ghosh of giving it away.

In the pause that followed, Elizabeth could be heard sobbing.

"How the mighty are fallen," Catherine said in English, giving her sister a sour look. "Pipe down for the lord's sake, Lizzie. You are always calling Fanny a prissy weakling, but she held up better in the forest than you did. Your bark is certainly worse than your bite."

"Young ladies," Pushpa said, "This is hardly the time to squabble. Remember that you are supposed to be members of a superior race. Your behavior right now suggests otherwise."

Catherine regretted her words. Fear and fatigue had brought her almost to the end of her tether. She must get a grip on herself. She set her lips grimly.

"If the rebels hear that four foreigners are hiding in the village," Mr. Ghosh said thoughtfully, "they will of course come looking for a group of four. So the first thing we shall do is to split the girls up. Two will stay here with us, and we will send the others elsewhere."

"Absolutely," Pushpa added. She seemed to be getting into the spirit of the thing. "Catherine must stay here. And little as I like the prospect of entertaining such a crybaby, I can see that Elizabeth must stay with us as well."

Elizabeth shot Pushpa a look of pure hatred.

Catherine heaved a sigh of relief, but forced herself to protest. "Why it must be Jane and Fanny who go to poor hut for sufferings? Why is it not being Elizabeth and me?" she asked. How she wished her spoken Hindi wasn't quite so awful.

"Once I read a story about a stolen letter," Pusha answered, surprisingly. "The criminal put it out in plain sight, among other letters in a letter holder. When the police came to look for it, they assumed that he would have hidden it. So they searched inside the books, under the floorboards, and so forth—but they never looked in the letter holder. We will hide Elizabeth and Catherine the same way, in plain sight."

"What a ridiculous idea," Elizabeth said. She was so pleased to be able to contradict that odious Pushpa that she forgot to speak in Hindi.

"Not at all," Pushpa said. "You and Catherine are both dark-haired. Dressed in *saris*, you could probably pass for Indians. While the *sepoys* who come to find you are looking under the beds and in the cupboards, you will go about your business like members of our household. If we're lucky, it won't occur to them to look at you closely. Like the policemen in the story, they will search for a clever hiding place — and when they can't find it, they will go away."

Elizabeth was silenced, but she did not look convinced.

"Yes, my children," Mr. Ghosh said thoughtfully, "That is a good plan. As for the other two girls, Jane and Fanny, they must go to live with the Simha family. The Simhas are better off than some of our villagers."

"I see what you have in mind," Komal added, "Jane and Fanny must wear ragged clothes and work in the fields with the Simhas. If *sepoys* come, they must pull their *dupattas* over their faces like modest peasant girls. In this way, they too will be hidden in plain sight. With Shiva's aid, this plan may save them."

"I am sorry, Komal," Mr. Ghosh said, "but you must leave Murarmau and go to Devender in Arjunabad. Perhaps he can help you rejoin Mrs. May. Our peasants will keep silent about the girls if I ask them to. But it will be hard for our small village to feed even four extra mouths. You would be the fifth. There is nothing to be gained by your staying."

"*I will go,*" Komal said sadly.

"We too will do what you advise," Jane added. "And we offer you a million thanks."

Jane's Hindi was much better than Catherine's, and she enjoyed showing it off. But she was not pleased to hear that she would be living with a peasant family.

Catherine wondered why Pushpa and Mr. Ghosh were so sure that the villagers would not betray her and her sisters if rebel *sepoys* came looking for them. After all, the villagers were Indians, and it had become utterly clear during the last horrible week that most Indians hated the English from the bottom of their hearts.

Papa thought the natives loved him, but Catherine was now sure he was fooling himself about that. Perhaps Mr. Ghosh was suffering from similar delusions. He was a *zamindar*—and why should dirt-poor peasants be loyal to their landlord? When Catherine thought of the pathetic huts the villagers lived in, she was convinced that they must hate Mr. Ghosh almost as much as they hated the English.

But Catherine saw no point in voicing her doubts. Pushpa and her father were clearly in charge, and they were now presenting a united front. Mr. Ghosh stood erect, with his arm around his daughter. His hand rested lightly on Mahendra's head. His silver hair glowed like a halo.

The sisters embraced Komal sorrowfully, as she went to get ready for her journey. She was the last link with their old life and she was leaving them.

CHAPTER THIRTEEN: IN A PEASANT'S HUT

A few hours later, the May girls were dressed in *saris* that Pushpa had found for them.

Catherine's and Elizabeth's were silk, not very elaborate, but pretty nonetheless. Catherine sighed. She would have to be careful not to wreck this valuable outfit. It had come from Pushpa's own wardrobe.

Elizabeth wished that anyone but Pushpa had given her this disguise. She couldn't bear to owe anything to that horrible woman. But there was nothing to be done about it. The only thing she could do was to loathe Pushpa until her dying day. And so she would. Angrily, she jerked the folds of her *sari* into place.

For Jane and Fanny, Pushpa had found tattered cotton *saris* of no particular color, castoffs from the Ghoshes' servants. She was just in time to save them from being torn into dust cloths.

Jane shuddered at the thought that Lieutenant Palliser might come to rescue her while she was wearing this awful garment, if you could even call it a garment. Not only was it extremely unbecoming, but it actually revealed her entire midriff.

Fanny caught Jane's eye. She wished that Jane had been chosen to stay with the Ghoshes instead of Catherine. Then Jane could have played dress up in a pink silk *sari* with a blue border, like the one Catherine was now wearing. And Catherine could literally have been dressed, as Jane often claimed she preferred, in rags. It would have been better for both of them.

Fanny was almost certain she felt lice crawling about in

her own *sari.* She could only hope she was imagining it. She began humming under her breath, "Jesus loves me, that I know." After a few minutes, she felt a bit better.

Mr. Ghosh gave Jane and Fanny each a bundle to carry. In a courtly manner, he guided them across the bazaar. Jane's heart sank as she realized that their destination was a small and tumbledown shack. She had been hoping for something different, since the Simhas were supposed to be more prosperous than most of the villagers. Even little Fanny had to stoop to get through the low doorway of this disgraceful hut.

Inside the shack, a youngish woman was tending several small pots over a charcoal fire. There was no chimney and the room was smoky. On a bench against the wall sat a handsome man and two lovely children with jet-black hair and eyes. The oldest, a girl, was about nine. The boy was two or three.

Jane stifled a cough and looked about curiously. Thank heaven, the room was not completely squalid. The dirt floor was swept clean, bedding was rolled up neatly in one corner, and bags of foodstuffs were stacked near a big grinding stone.

The Simhas wore coarse, faded clothing, not much better than the *saris* she and Fanny had been given. Yet you couldn't really say they were in rags—and certainly they were not starving. An appetizing smell came from the pots on the fire and the little boy might even be called plump. At least by Indian standards.

All four Simhas rose at the sight of Mr. Ghosh. Mrs. Simha bent down respectfully and touched the *zamindar*'s feet with her forehead.

Mr. Ghosh asked her to care for the two foreigners. She agreed without hesitation. When Mr. Ghosh told her of the dangers involved, Mrs. Simha smiled.

"*Zamindar,*" she said respectfully, "You are our father and mother. You have given us our lives, and we must give them back to you should the need arise. There is no more to say."

Mr. Simha nodded.

Jane was surprised. Were these peasants just currying favor with their landlord — or was something more at work here? The Simhas even seemed pleased that Mr. Ghosh had asked for their help.

"This is Kasthuri and this is Krishna," Mr. Ghosh said, pointing to the two children. "And this is Madam Fanny and Madam Jane. Young ladies, Mrs. Simha will tell you what to do. Obey her slightest word and you will be safe enough."

With a quick smile, he disappeared.

"You took the dust of the *zamindar's* feet," Mr. Simha said to his wife in an outraged tone, "yet you never pay me such a mark of respect. Does not a wife owe reverence to her husband? Should he not be as a god to her?"

"No sane woman could mistake you for a god," Mrs. Simha retorted. "I pay respect only where it is due. When you have become as wise a man as the *zamindar,* I will touch your feet indeed. Meanwhile, you are the worst farmer in the village and you hardly know the difference between a cow and a bull. Count yourself lucky that I give you houseroom!"

But Mrs. Simha's affectionate tone contradicted her harsh words. She turned back to the stove and soon finished her cooking.

Her husband followed her movements with hungry eyes.

Mrs. Simha handed everyone some rice and *dal* on a rough wooden plate. For several seconds, Fanny looked in vain for a fork. Then she saw that the Simhas were scooping up their food with their fingers or with small pieces of *chapatti*. Quickly, she fixed her eyes on her own plate. She hoped Mrs. Simha hadn't noticed her hesitation or guessed the reason for it. How shaming that would be for the poor woman.

But Fanny couldn't quite bear to eat such gooey food with her hand, and the rice seemed to flee as she chased it with a bit of *chapatti*. She was mortified when she had several near accidents. She felt relieved that no second helpings were offered.

When they were done eating, Mr. Simha returned to his bench, where he sat staring vacantly at the wall. Pulling their *dupattas* over their hair, Fanny and Jane went to the *ghat* with the rest of the family to wash the cooking pots. A crowd of village women was there, doing the same thing.

Mrs. Simha told the women why the sisters were staying with her family. Everyone seemed to accept their presence. No one complained about the danger. Once again, Jane saw that Mr. Ghosh's will was law in the village.

CHAPTER FOURTEEN: LITTLE PEASANTS

The next day, the Simhas arose at first light. Mr. Simha immediately left the hut.

Fanny thought he was probably answering what Mama delicately referred to as "a call of nature." At home, when she had to relieve herself, Fanny went into the bathroom, shut the door, and used the commode. A sweeper always sat outside the room, ready to empty the porcelain bowl as soon as Fanny was finished. Papa liked to call the commode a thunder box. This joke about the noises people made while using it struck Fanny as disgusting. Not funny at all.

The Simhas certainly didn't have a bathroom or a commode. God only knew what they did when nature called, but Fanny would have to find out.

"What do you do when you have to...?" she asked Mrs. Simha, gesturing toward the doorway through which Mr. Simha had disappeared.

"Do you really need my aid to solve this mighty problem?" Mrs. Simha said with a smile. "Have the civilized ways that foreigners are so proud of chased away all your common sense? Go into the jungle, squat down, and wipe yourself with leaves or the edge of a rock when you are done."

How could she possibly obey these directions? Fanny wondered. What was to stop a cobra or a scorpion from biting her on the bum? And what if someone spied on her? A horrible thought, but then, she really had no choice.

Mrs. Simha sat down on the bench with little Krishna

on her lap. Slipping her *sari* off her shoulder, she gave the child her breast. Fanny had never seen such a thing. How awful. Nursing a baby was bad enough, but to do it with a boy who was old enough to chatter like a magpie was positively against nature. Well, perhaps not against nature, but it was certainly uncivilized. Suppose he complained about the taste—how embarrassing.

Fanny blushed deeply and looked away. She wasn't sure she could endure life with the Simhas. But of course she would try. Papa, Mama, Komal, and Mr. Ghosh would all expect her to do her very best. So when Mrs. Simha put Krishna down, Fanny quickly asked if she could help her cook.

"Not now," Mrs. Simha answered. "We eat only twice a day. And it is very lucky that things are no worse. We must all do our morning's work before we break our fast. One of you will stay here and help Kasthuri do the housework. The other must help me in the fields since my husband does not do farm work. Which will it be?"

Fanny opened her mouth to volunteer for the harder job, but Jane forestalled her.

"I will work in the fields," she said firmly.

She couldn't let her little sister toil in the brutal Indian sun, while she did household tasks indoors. Fanny was only a child, but she herself was almost grown up. If her skin turned black and neither Lieutenant Palliser nor James Keats wanted to marry her, so be it.

Fanny looked a bit miffed at the way Jane had balked her good intentions.

"Can I not help Mr. Simha his work?" she asked in halting Hindi. Despite her difficulties with the language, she managed to produce her habitual self-denying tone.

"When my husband goes to the forest, you may help him there. But he does not do this often. On many days he stays at home and looks after Krishna."

"Why does he not help you in the fields?" Jane asked curiously.

"Though he is of our caste, a cultivator caste, he was raised among the forest nomads," Mrs. Simha answered, "And I have not managed to teach him how to farm. He is not a quick learner. I often say that he was a cockroach in his previous life, and he brought its tiny brain with him to his incarnation as a man. If I ask him to weed, he pulls up the grain—and the weeds flourish as if they had been blessed by a higher power. It is easier to farm without his so-called help. Kasthuri replaces me at home. But it will be good to have one of you to help me."

She smiled at Jane, carefully shouldered a gleaming sickle, and left for the fields.

Mrs. Simha explained that she herself would reap the ripe grain. Jane would follow behind, collecting armfuls of the cut stalks and binding them into sheaves. Mrs. Simha described this as an easy task. Jane rolled her eyes.

The patch they were harvesting was one of those which had looked weedy to Catherine, accustomed as she was to England's uniform fields of wheat or barley. But it now turned out that this patch had been sown with a mixture of barley and lentils on purpose. Mrs. Simha explained that if bad weather ruined the barley, the lentils, which could handle harsh conditions, might survive. Jane saw that it was a kind of insurance.

Jane pulled up her ragged *dupatta* in hopes of preventing her skin from tanning, but it soon became clear that this would not do. She needed both hands for her work, and if she did not hold it in place, the length of cloth slipped off her head.

After an hour, Jane's throat was parched. She felt light headed from hunger. Her aching back screamed for help. Just as she was about to demand a rest break, Mrs. Simha told her it was time to go home for *chota hazri.*

As they walked back from the field, Mrs. Simha said, "You have done well for the first day. You learn quickly, and your hands are nimble. Soon you will be a good farmer."

Jane glowed with pleasure. She was happy that this competent woman did not see her as a reincarnated cockroach. Or even as a charming little kitten, like Villette Heathcliff in Catherine's play. She felt a bit sorry for Mr. Simha, sitting idly at home.

Jane was amazed at how quickly she gained strength. At the end of a fortnight, she spent a whole morning dipping up water from the river in a big, shallow basket called a *behri* and dumping it into a sloping ditch that irrigated the recently planted fall crop of millet. Not even the superhuman Mrs. Simha could call this a light task. Jane's arms felt as if she would never be able to lift them again. Back at the hut, she attacked her rice and *dal* with incredible appetite.

Walking towards the river a few days later, Jane noticed that her hands were no longer their usual shade of tender pink. They were now a warm brown color. Not too bad, she decided, though the calluses on her palms were a bit distressing. Had the sun turned her perfect nose red, like Susan Brown's? The Simhas didn't own a mirror, so she couldn't check. But if it had, it had. Jane flexed her right arm and was surprised to see a muscle rise beneath her smooth skin. Surely that muscle was new development? She smiled as she bent down to fill the *behri*.

While she worked, Jane began to wonder about the Simhas' finances. Papa often said that the Company taxed its peasants very moderately, using the most scientific methods to decide how much each family could afford to pay.

That sounded sensible enough. But if the taxes were really so fair and moderate, why didn't the Simhas have enough food to eat three times a day? Why was their bedding so ragged and their hut not even weatherproof? Why did they have only one bullock for plowing? Their few small cooking pots were blackened and dented.

Jane felt that her own Hindi was not yet up to discussing economics. When it improved, she would ask Mrs. Simha about all this. Mrs. Simha was illiterate, but she was also very shrewd. Jane felt sure that she would be able to explain.

For the first few days at the Simhas', Fanny helped

Kasthuri clean and cook. She learned to measure spices by eye and to grind them to perfection in the stone mortar. She learned to build a charcoal fire that was just big enough to cook a meal. She learned how long to boil the *dal*. She learned that a twig broom works well for cleaning a dirt floor. She learned how to eat very neatly *without* a fork.

In fact, there was no end to the number of things she had to learn. She was amazed at little Kasthuri's knowledge. The child had inherited her mother's intelligence. And it was a good thing, too, because the family could never have managed without Kasthuri's labor.

Fanny's own labor was also needed, she could see, desperately needed, now that the family had two extra members. She threw herself into the work. At home Fanny had always tried to make sacrifices for the good of others, but she sometimes felt that her sacrifices weren't particularly necessary. She never felt that way at the Simhas'.

Of course, there was the occasional setback.

"Madam Fanny," Kasthuri said, "We have run out of charcoal. Tomorrow you must go to the forest with my father to help him make more. And to collect some other things as well. Meanwhile, we must burn dung. Please go pick some up."

Fanny was not pleased with this assignment, but she obediently took a basket and went outside. There stood the family's bullock. Mrs. Simha had christened him "*Gur*," the Hindi word for molasses, because he moved so slowly.

Gur's droppings were scattered about. Some were distressingly fresh, some old and dried out. Deciding that fresh materials are generally preferable to decayed ones, Fanny fought down her disgust and filled her basket with the wettest dung she could find. Shuddering from head to foot, she poured some water from a clay pot over her hands. Then she carried the basket indoors, proud to have executed an unpleasant task exceptionally well.

Kasthuri took one look and laughed. "Oh, Madam Fanny, how silly you are. How could you think wet dung would burn? Do you not know that water puts out fire? I think you must have a tiny cockroach brain like my father's. You must empty this basket on the manure pile and pick up the driest cowpats you can find."

Blushing with embarrassment, Fanny did as she was told. Then she and Kasthuri cautiously built a small fire and began toasting spices. The dry dung burned well, but smoked far more horribly than charcoal. Acrid fumes stung Fanny's eyes.

"Stop, stop, Madam Fanny," Kasthuri cried as Fanny, coughing convulsively, took a pot of moong *dal* off the fire. "The dung does not make such a hot fire as the charcoal. So you must cook everything longer. Put the pot back on the fire. I will finish the cooking."

Something else to remember! Fanny sighed and went to play cat's cradle with Krishna. She adored the cuddly little fellow. She loved it when he called her "my new mama." And she was glad Kasthuri had taken over the cooking. She didn't think she could bear another humiliation today. She devoutly hoped there was nothing she ought to be doing instead of playing with Krishna. Because if there were, she just wasn't going to do it.

But by the next day, Fanny's conscience was bothering her again. Was she really helping the Simhas as much as she should? So when Mrs. Simha asked her to go into the forest with Mr. Simha, Fanny agreed eagerly, even though it meant spending the day away from Krishna. She had no idea what, besides making charcoal, they were going to do there.

Krishna howled when his two favorite playmates got ready to leave the hut. Fanny snatched him up and buried her nose in his marvelously soft neck. Soon he was giggling ecstatically. It took so little to make him happy. She promised to play "bazaar" with him when she got home. He loved selling her piles of stones in exchange for piles of leaves.

Mr. Simha carried an axe and a shovel in a big basket. He had a coil of rope slung over his shoulder. Never one to waste words, he led Fanny toward the forest in total silence. He kept looking back over his shoulder as if he was afraid of being seen. Why on earth was he afraid? But it was still very early and no one appeared.

Soon Mr. Simha left the path and scrambled through the underbrush. Fanny followed, wondering where they might be going. The forest pulsated noisily, like a huge beast with a bad head cold. An insect or perhaps a lizard kept up a regular metallic chirping. Mr. Simha pushed on without hesitation. Now it was Fanny who kept glancing back over her shoulder.

They finally arrived at an open glade surrounded by a stand of deodar and oak. A few flame-of- the-forest trees, with their brilliant red blossoms, dotted the clearing. Rows of black fruit bats, each the size of a lap dog, hung from the branches. Fanny shuddered as she reminded herself that these repulsive creatures would not wake up until sunset.

She noticed that a lot of branches had been lopped off the oak trees and laid on the ground to dry.

Taking his axe from the basket, Mr. Simha chopped these dry branches into sticks of even length. Using the blunt end of the axe blade as a hammer, he drove four of the straightest sticks into the ground, making a small square.

"*Chimney*," he said in tones of satisfaction. Fanny had no idea what he meant.

He began to pile lengths of wood around the square space marked out by the four stakes. He made signs that Fanny was to do the same. Soon the empty square space was surrounded and covered by an igloo shaped pile of wood. Fanny now saw that space enclosed by the vertical stakes actually did resemble a chimney.

In building the wooden igloo, Mr. Simha had left an open tunnel running along the ground toward the chimney at the igloo's center. By reaching in through the tunnel, a person *could* build a small fire at the bottom of the chimney.

But unlike an ordinary chimney, the top of this one was not open. In fact, it was completely covered by the pieces of wood that formed the rounded top of the igloo. Who ever heard of a chimney with a lid? Mr. Simha's proceedings seemed crazy to Fanny.

She wondered if Mrs. Simha had been flattering her husband when she said he knew his way around the forest. Perhaps Mrs. Simha couldn't bear the thought that her husband was a total fool, as useless in the jungle as he was on a farm. No, that was unlikely. Mrs. Simha was usually *quite* reliable. She had a truly *masculine* grasp of logic and fact. And she certainly wasn't inclined to flatter her husband.

"*Mud,*" Mr. Simha said, gesturing expansively with his shovel. He began digging up damp earth. He showed Fanny how to plaster it over the igloo.

This took some time. Just when Fanny thought they would never be done, Mr. Simha took a step backwards.

"*Finished,*" he said proudly, gazing with adoration at the igloo, which now looked like a huge lump of mud.

Spurred on by his achievement, he added, "In the field I am no better than a woman, but in the forest, I am a man."

Mr. Simha put some bits of brushwood in the bottom of the chimney, took a flint from the basket, and struck a spark. Soon the brushwood was burning. He piled sticks in front of the tunnel leading into the igloo, almost closing off its entrance.

Fanny looked at him in disbelief.

"Won't the fire go out?" she asked. "You've cut off the air supply completely."

"No, you are mistaken. There is still some air," Mr. Simha told her. "The fire sucks it in through the tunnel. But very little comes in. For this reason, the fire will burn up the pile of wood very, very slowly. And that is what we want. In five days the wood will have turned into best quality charcoal. Then we will return and put out the fire."

Perhaps Mr. Simha actually does understand forestry, Fanny thought. At any rate, he seems to know how to make charcoal. But he *is* a slow learner in general. And that's got to be upsetting for his wife.

Fanny couldn't imagine why Mrs. Simha constantly called attention to her husband's stupidity by joking about it. Wouldn't she be better off trying to ignore it? To encourage the children to respect their father by treating him respectfully herself? Yes, surely that would be a better way to manage the situation.

In Fanny's opinion, jokes were usually distressing. She hated to think of the reason her father called the commode a "thunder box." And even if they didn't involve references to such improper matters, jokes were always based on exaggeration and distortion. Joking could *not* be reconciled with the duty to tell the exact truth! Fanny never joked, and she rarely laughed when other people tried to be funny.

But thinking about the Simhas now, she wondered. Mrs. Simha's jokes certainly exaggerated Mr. Simha's stupidity. He wasn't by any means an idiot. But could it be that joking about his stupidity helped Mrs. Simha to deal with it? Perhaps failings seemed *less* serious if you could laugh at them?

Mr. Simha put his tools in the basket and left the clearing with a manly stride. His success with the charcoal operation had certainly boosted his confidence.

"We will now fill our basket with bark from the bhojpatra tree, Madam Fanny. Flattened out, this bark can be used for many things. It can be used as paper or to make umbrellas for the monsoon season. We do not need umbrellas right now, though we will need them soon. But we need the bark we are taking today immediately. We will use it to cover the patches of rice that my wife has just planted. The cover warms the tiny plants and so helps them grow."

"Is it difficult to take off bark without the tree hurting?" Fanny asked. As she spoke, she realized that her Hindi was definitely improving.

"It is man's work," Mr. Simha said proudly. "Very difficult indeed. No woman can do it well. But there is no man to help me, so I must make do with you."

He shot Fanny a look as if daring her to contradict him. His wife would undoubtedly have done so, but he had nothing to fear from Fanny. She pitied him even more when he tried to assert himself than when he sat on his bench gazing into the fire.

Fanny was not surprised when the bark stripping process proved fairly easy to learn. Soon the basket was full and nothing remained but to carry it home. The sun had just set when they reached the edge of the forest.

CHAPTER FIFTEEN: OUTLAW FANNY

Mrs. Simha welcomed them home with a look of relief that puzzled Fanny. Taking the basket from her husband's hands, she motioned them to sit down and immediately served their food. As they ate, she stood by attentively.

"Today you are behaving like a true wife," Mr. Simha said in approving tones. "Until the husband has eaten, the wife should remain fasting. But this is not the way you usually act. Often you have swallowed your entire meal before I take a single bite."

"That is because I have far more work than you do," she answered in her usual sharp manner. "If I stood waiting for you to stop nibbling like a *maharajah* before I ate, I would need the aid of a higher power to get through all my tasks. But today I was worried about you and Madam Fanny. I have no appetite."

"Why were you worried?" Jane asked, thinking of the snakes, tigers, and wild boars that lurked in the jungle. Fanny's safety had been on her own mind all day.

"Because the English have turned the forest into what they call a reserved area," Mrs. Simha answered surprisingly. "This means that we can no longer go there to make charcoal, pick up fallen leaves for mulch, or strip bark from the bhoj-patra tree—things that our people have done time out of mind. If they catch us doing these things, they say we have broken their law, and they send us to jail."

"But surely you can get along without doing these things?" Fanny said.

She couldn't believe that the Company made rules that harmed the peasants. Good men like Papa wouldn't stand for it. A lump rose in Fanny's throat as she thought about Papa. Where were he and Mama now? Did they ever think of her? Were they even alive? Would they ever know how hard she was trying to help the Simhas?

"No, Madam Fanny, we cannot," Mrs. Simha said sadly. "We are poor people and we need the forest. If we cannot cut branches and make charcoal, we must burn dung, as you have seen. But if we burn our dung, we do not have it to fertilize our fields. No, no, we cannot farm without the forest. Then too, we make medicines from its plants. We gather fruits and nuts. Oh, the list of things the forest gives us is truly endless."

"Then why did the Company make this law?" Fanny asked, her voice trailing off miserably.

As usual, Mrs. Simha was at no loss for an answer.

"The Company says that the forests belong to them. They want tall straight trees for shipbuilding. They say that if we lop branches for charcoal, this makes the trees knotty and stunts their growth. They also say that charcoal burning starts fires, which destroy the big trees. This is why they want to keep us out of the forests."

Fanny didn't like to disagree with an adult, even an Indian adult, but she felt she had to defend the Company.

"Aren't those good reasons?" she said. "After all,

British ships are needed for trade and trade adds to the prosperity of India."

"Prosperity indeed," Mrs. Simha retorted angrily. "Where is this famous prosperity? We Indians see none of it! We die like flies in famines. Starving parents sell their children. If they can find anyone to buy! A stark-naked sadhu with a begging bowl eats better than a hard working peasant. And this is not to say that the sadhu eats well!"

"But surely the peasants wouldn't want to start forest fires if they really need the forest as much as you say? If charcoal burning starts fires, I should think they'd be better off not doing it," Jane said.

"Not at all. The fires burn down the tall trees, but they also clear a space for new trees to grow. The English want the biggest trees for their big ships, but small timber is more useful to us. It is easier to handle, and it is just as good for making charcoal. The leaves of many small trees mulch our fields as well as the leaves of one big tree."

It wasn't easy to win an argument with Mrs. Simha, Jane thought, not for the first time.

"The Company cannot turn something we have always done into a crime," Mrs. Simha said. "This is a simple truth, but the English do not understand it. What good is their education if it does not teach them we will do what we must do to survive? Their heads have room for only one idea at a time — if that. And now their idea is that they must have ships."

"Yes, it is a disgrace," her husband said in excited

tones. "I have been jailed. I have been placed on the police list like a common thief. And what did they catch me doing in the forest? What was my crime? Collecting dry grass to feel poor old Gur, whose belly was as empty as a rain barrel before the monsoon!"

Jane was surprised. She had never heard Mr. Simha say more than a few words about anything—except his wife's unfeminine behavior. On that subject, he held forth like Papa preaching to his daughters about self-sacrifice! Whether they were Indian or English, men seemed to enjoy telling women how to behave.

"If you have gotten into trouble for breaking these new rules," she asked Mr. Simha, "why did you go into the forest today? Weren't you afraid of being caught?"

"Yes, we are afraid," Mrs. Simha said. It was her habit to answer questions addressed to her husband. "My husband has not gone into the forest for many weeks. He has been sitting idly at home, as you know. But we need many things. I hoped that it would be safe now."

"*Why was that?*" Fanny asked.

"The English are fighting the **sepoys**. I think they will not patrol the forests around Murarmau until the rebellion is over. So I told my husband that he could go."

Jane nodded sympathetically.

But Fanny did not feel very sympathetic. She was horrified to learn that she had spent the entire day breaking the Company's laws. The entire day! She of all people! She was angry, well almost angry, at Mrs. Simha for placing her in such a position. Suppose she had been caught! How embarrassing for the daughter of a magistrate! How upset dear Papa would have been to hear what she had done! How displeased he would have been with her.

Fanny was sure that everyone had a duty to obey the law. Ignorance of the law was no excuse for disobedience. What could be clearer than that?

But still... the Simhas were very poor. As Mrs. Simha said, they needed the forest. And his forest skills were Mr. Simha's whole life, the only source of pride he had. Did the Company have a right to take the forest away from him? To make him sit indoors on a bench feeling inferior to his wife.

A startling question popped into Fanny's mind. Would she really have refused to go with Mr. Simha today if she had known that charcoal making was illegal? Perhaps not. No, certainly not. She would never have let the Simhas down like that. She couldn't bear to think of Krishna going hungry.

"I wish you had told me beforehand," Fanny said slowly, "but I am glad I was able to help."

"We did not tell you beforehand because I thought that you might refuse," Mrs. Simha said. "And I see that this was wrong. I should not have put you in danger without your consent. I will not do this again. There is no more to say."

Fanny also felt that there was no more to say. But there was much to think about. A grown-up had apologized to her. She couldn't remember that this had ever happened before. She had never heard Papa admit that he was wrong. Until today she had assumed that this was because he was always right. Now she wasn't so sure.

Taking Krishna on her lap, Fanny kissed his black curls. She remembered the many starving children with sticklike limbs and swollen bellies she had seen in the slums of Shivapur. No, she would never let that happen to Krishna if she could prevent it.

Lying on her thin mat that night, Jane had trouble falling asleep, despite her long day in the fields. She rolled from side to side. She couldn't believe that Fanny had actually sided with the Simhas in their resistance to the Company. It seemed completely out of character.

"Are you awake, Jane?" Fanny whispered in English.

"Well, sort of," her sister answered.

"I'm sorry to bother you. I know how hard you've been working. But I simply have to ask you something. Today I broke the law. And if Mrs. Simha asks me to do it again, I am going to say yes. Do you think God will send me to hell for that—like an ordinary criminal?"

"I'm not sure, Fanny," Jane said honestly.

"Papa says we should be selfless," Fanny added. "And he thinks that selfishness is unwomanly. I always thought it would be easy to tell the difference."

"Isn't it?" Jane asked. "I should say it's very selfless of you to break the law for the Simhas' sake. I can see that you're feeling terrible pangs of conscience, and what could be more selfless than to suffer terrible pangs for the sake of others?"

"Oh, Jane, you know that pangs of conscience are the one kind of suffering Papa *wouldn't* want us to seek out. And you know just as well that commiting crimes isn't what he has in mind when he says we should do unpleasant things in order to help others."

"No, I suppose not. But I still think it's generous of you to put yourself through all this guilt for Krishna's sake."

"But am I *really* being generous? *I* would suffer a lot if I had to see Krishna suffering. So maybe it's selfish of me to try to prevent that. Oh, I'm so confused. Papa's principles don't seem to be guiding me as well as I thought they would."

"Living with the Simhas has made a lot of things look different to me, too," Jane said in comforting tones. "I thought Mrs. Simha had a point when she said that the rule you and Mr. Simha broke was unjust. So perhaps you should simply tell your conscience to stop bothering you."

"I couldn't do that. The Company's laws may not be perfect, but surely they're not so *very* unjust that we can disobey them with a clear conscience. No, taking things from the Company's forests is definitely stealing! I have to face that. It seems almost unfair of God to put me in such an impossible position. But of course I shouldn't criticize Him."

There was a long pause.

"In fact," Fanny added, in her habitual self-denying tone, "if it should be God's will to damn me for stealing when I know that stealing is wrong, I'll just have to go to hell."

"I hope it won't come to that," Jane told her soothingly.

Fanny felt better now that she had faced the worst. She soon fell asleep, but Jane did not.

As Jane flopped about restlessly, she heard an unusual noise from the other end of the room. There were scuffling sounds, and then Mr. Simha began grunting in a very peculiar way. Jane was sure the strange noises he was making were not snores. A few moments later, Mrs. Simha started moaning. In almost no time, she was practically screeching.

Jane was about to go to Mrs. Simha's aid when a new idea made her hestitate.

Mrs. May had wished to keep her daughters ignorant of everything related to human reproduction. But she hadn't been completely successful. As she told her husband, it had unfortunately been necessary to give the girls some information in the interests of hygiene. Then too, there were animals all over the place, going about their business without the slightest concern for propriety. To make matters worse, the Bible was often shockingly frank. All those awful verses about who begat whom.

Jane remembered that her mother, gesturing vaguely, had told her never to touch a certain part of her own body. And she recalled something almost unbelievable that Ellen Barnfather had told her about what Ellen referred to as "marital relations." Now Jane put two and two together. She decided that she had better stay where she was.

The image of Lieutenant Palliser sitting gracefully on his horse stole into Jane's mind as Mrs. Simha's cries subsided. She could see his slim hands holding the reins. She buried her hot face in her arms.

CHAPTER SIXTEEN: AT THE GHOSHES'

Catherine wrote in her notebook:

"Notebook, I have decided to use you as a diary. From now on, I will address you simply as 'Diary.'

We have been in Murarmau almost two weeks. Today is May 30th. Have seen no **sepoys** yet. Thanks be to the gods of some religion or other! But news of mutiny (or perhaps should call it rebellion?) comes here via famous 'jungle telegraph.' So we know that our army marched out of Meerut to take Delhi back from rebels. They failed and are now camped on a ridge near the city. Mughal emperor Zafar has joined rebels. Mr. Ghosh—who knows *all* about politics—says Zafar had no choice. Rebels must have threatened him. Whatever. Fact remains: situation up in air.

Worried about Ali and James. Ali quite capable of running away to join rebels. Not sure what James will do. Can only hope he is still in Malior. Also hope aged parents made it to Meerut. Should be safe there. But, oh dear, suppose Papa had relapse and couldn't flee to Meerut? Perhaps we are not safe here either, but somehow can't feel frightened. Everything is so peaceful. So bucolic. How do you like that big word, Diary?

It turns out there is a Mrs. Ghosh. Hard to believe Pushpa actually *has* a mother. Pushpa seems to have sprung full grown from forehead of Jove. She is so strong. Mrs. Ghosh not equally strong. Is always complaining. She told me, in Hindi of course: *'I wept a monsoon when I saw I would never have a son. I wept a river when Pushpa disgraced me by marrying a foreigner. But when Mahin came to us I stopped weeping. Such a beautiful boy. I make him milk sweets so he will grow up strong. I rub ghee into his hair so it will shine. But even as I am working my fingers to the bone for Mahin, my husband is giving our money right and left to the peasants.'*

The day I got here, Pushpa also said something about her father giving away Mahin's inheritance. Wonder what this can mean. Peasants in Murarmau definitely not rich! But wouldn't they be rich if Mr. Ghosh had given them all his money?

Dear Diary, prepare for big surprise: I get along very well with Mrs. Ghosh. As you know, am used to scatty mothers. So can manage them easily. And Mrs. G. is as scatty as Mama, though in different ways. I tell Mrs. G. she is best wife, mother, and grandmother ever seen in universe. Without exceptions. Also tell her Mahin is most utterly brilliant, well-behaved, handsome boy ever born. Oddly enough, there is some truth in this. Mrs. G. thinks about her family all the time. Is very respectful to Mr. G., though can't stop self from criticizing him behind his back. Keeps house immaculate and cooks most delicious things. Is very religious. Performs endless prayers to large collection of gods every morning. As for Mahendra, he really is a sweetie pie.

Because Mrs. G. likes me, Mr. G. asked me to keep her company and help with household tasks she won't trust to servants. So am learning much about making milk sweets. For example, I spend hours stirring pan of boiling milk with big wooden spatula. Finally it turns to sticky golden mass. Oh, how good it smells. Mrs. G. shows me right moment to pour it onto a board, where it firms up into something called *khoa*. But that's just the beginning. Mrs. G. tells me we will make this *khoa* into *tilkuta* for Mahin. What is *tilkuta*, I ask self? No worries. Mrs. G. will soon show me. We fry sesame seeds and coconut in ghee, and then knead them into the *khoa* along with sugar and cardamom and yet more ghee. Then cook it all together until it forms a ball. Let it cool and divide into many smaller balls. Fry *more* sesame seeds in ghee. Roll each ball in seeds. Can't quite believe how much ghee we're using!

Process of making *tilkuta* almost as complicated as *Mrs. Seaton*'s mad laundry routine. But Mrs. G. has whole thing in her head. No recipes needed—which is just as well, because she cannot read. Mrs. G. would like Mahin to eat *all* the *tilkuta*, but forces self to offer me some. I take three quickly, before she changes mind. Delicious. But very, very sweet. No wonder Mrs. G. so plump.

Didn't, alas, manage to keep *sari* quite clean through all this.

Mrs. G. tells me that tomorrow she will teach me to make sweet called *jalebi*. Says *jalebis* much more difficult to make than 'simple' *tilkuta* made today. I shudder.

In this way, Diary, days have been passing. Feel more like Indian housewife than writer. But tell self that Currer Bell kept house for her father and wrote too! *Must* jot down everything that happens here, as it may provide basis for novel about mutiny—though must admit that so far have only been on fringes of mutiny. Perhaps novel about Indian life, then?

Mr. G. says Jane and Fanny are well. I miss Fanny a lot. But am sure she is being useful to Simha family. Can't imagine 'vain Jane' living like a peasant. No pretty clothes, no admirers. Maybe not even enough food? Feel sorry for her. Elizabeth seems all right, but am so busy with Mrs. G. that haven't seen her much."

In fact, Elizabeth spent her first few days with the

Ghoshes brooding in silence. She had no drawing materials, so she couldn't do the only thing that made her really happy. She didn't like children, and in any case, Mahendra was a very spoiled little boy. He consumed an unbelievable quantity of milk sweets. She tried to get him to moderate his gluttony by shooting many disapproving looks in his direction. It wouldn't be safe to chide him openly — though he certainly deserved it. Pushpa defended Mahendra like a tigress, even when he was clearly in the wrong.

It wasn't long before Pushpa intercepted one of these glares.

"You are living here on sufferance, Elizabeth," she snapped, omitting the honorific title "Madam." "You moon about doing nothing, and yet you grudge Mahin the food that his grandmother loves to make for him. A hard-working Indian woman like my mother is worth a dozen idle *memsahib*s like you!"

"If you want me to work, I will work," Elizabeth retorted. "But you have to tell me what to do. You ignore me. You don't want me here. You don't even see me as a person — I'm just one of those English devils you can't stop hating. You have no right, no right at all, to call me lazy!"

Anger seemed to be having a remarkably good effect on her Hindi.

Mr. Ghosh had been listening.

"Madam Elizabeth is right, daughter," he said in his usual calm tone. "She is suffering from boredom and anxiety. We must not be hard on her. Time will pass more quickly for her and she will be less irritable if she can stay busy."

"That's easy to say," Pushpa retorted, "but what can she do? She knows nothing, and unlike Catherine, she hasn't shown any wish to learn. She despises our ways."

Elizabeth was silent. There was some truth in what Pushpa had said. She wasn't proud of the way she'd behaved since the mutiny started. Breaking down on the march through the forest, surrendering to depression once they were safe in Murarmau. But she wouldn't give Pushpa the satisfaction of admitting it.

Mr. Ghosh had been thinking, and now he broke the silence.

"As it happens, today is the day when I must begin collecting the money that the peasants owe us. They have now had time to sell their spring crops. Madam Elizabeth can carry my ledger and record the payments. It will be good to have a literate person to help me. You have enough to do teaching Mahin, Pushpa, my dear."

Elizabeth felt better. Resolving to keep the ledger with unparalleled neatness and accuracy, if only to prove that Pushpa was wrong about her, she followed Mr. Ghosh into the hot sunshine.

"We will begin by visiting the peasants in the village," Mr. Ghosh told her. "Then we shall call on the ones who live further afield. Perhaps we should start with the Simhas, since your sisters are there. It will be a chance for you to see them."

Mr. Ghosh, Elizabeth reflected, thought about other people a lot. Whatever the situation, he tried to come up with a practical plan to deal with it. One that would please as many people as possible. He was good at that kind of planning, and he clearly enjoyed it. Not like that tiresome Fanny, who made pointless sacrifices just to prove how virtuous she was!

When they got to the Simhas' hut, the family was eating. Elizabeth embraced Jane eagerly. She embraced Fanny less eagerly. Tanned and strong, Jane looked more beautiful than ever. Fanny was as pale as usual, but her manner seemed less timid.

"Mr. Simha," Mr. Ghosh said, in a respectful tone, "I have come on an unpleasant mission. But it won't surprise you. Of course you remember that I loaned you a hundred rupees to pay the spring *kist*. Now I need you to repay the loan."

"Yes, *zamindar*, the repayment is ready. We have harvested and sold our spring crop."

"Madam Jane, Madam Fanny," Mrs. Simha added excitedly. "You cannot know what we owe the *zamindar*. The Company insists that our tax payment, which is called the *kist*, must be paid on the exact day it is due. But in both spring and autumn, the *kist* falls due before the crop can be harvested. And until we harvest and sell our crop, we have no money to pay the *kist*. Thus are we spitted on the horns of a dilemma."

"You will bore Madam Jane and Madam Fanny with this talk of money matters," Mr. Ghosh interrupted. But Mrs. Simha would not be stopped.

"No, you cannot silence me," she said, smiling. "The money for the *kist* has to be borrowed. If the *zamindar* did not advance us money to tide us over until the crops are sold, we would have to borrow it from the *bania*, the moneylender. For every rupee the *bania* lends, you must repay two. But Mr. Ghosh charges no interest."

"Goodness gracious," Jane asked, "how could you possibly pay interest at such a rate? You're barely getting by as it is."

"We couldn't. Nor can others who do not live in Murarmau. In other villages, where the *zamindar* does not help them, most peasants have debts they can never repay. Every year they owe the *bania* more than they did the year before! The *bania* lets them keep only enough grain to avoid starvation. They eat once a day, if that. They go almost naked. We are very poor, but we are not in debt, and we do not have to live like animals."

Mr. Ghosh looked uncomfortable. "No, no, Mrs. Simha," he said, "You are far too good a manager ever to be reduced to such poverty. I feel sure that you would always find a way to make ends meet."

"You may be right," Mrs. Simha retorted, "but *zamindar* though you are, I must say I do not agree. The peasant can never repay loans at high interest. In bad years, there is no crop to sell, and in good years, prices fall so low that selling the crop is hardly worthwhile. Without the aid of a higher power, which is rarely forthcoming, it cannot be done."

Mr. Ghosh was silent.

Elizabeth wondered if Mrs. Simha believed in God — or should she say, in the gods? Perhaps Mrs. Simha really was an unbeliever. Why else would she sneer at the idea that a higher power might come to the rescue of the starving peasants?

If this were true, then Mrs. Simha was the first person Elizabeth had ever met who shared her own deep skepticism. The English community believed firmly that an all-powerful God had sent his only begotten son down to earth on a mission of mercy. People who "had doubts" about this were spoken of in horrified tones, as if they "had" a disease like cholera.

But seeing all the suffering around her, Elizabeth had found it impossible *not* to doubt. Mrs. Simha's thoughts seemed to have followed the same path. And what did it mean to say that God had "begotten" a human son? A vision of God, stark naked, except for a long white beard, popped into Elizabeth's mind. She shook her head angrily and blushed.

CHAPTER SEVENTEEN: SAVING MR. GHOSH

As the days passed, Elizabeth and Mr. Ghosh visited the peasants who lived in the village. Many of them cheerfully repaid the money Mr. Ghosh had loaned them, just as the Simhas had. In her neatest handwriting, Elizabeth recorded their payments in the ledger. Under "Balance Owed," she wrote a big zero.

But others did not have the whole sum ready. They begged Mr. Ghosh to give them extra time. There were a variety of reasons.

The Patke family had married off their daughter, Sunita. Mr. Patke told Mr. Ghosh in despairing tones that they had been forced to cough up pots, pans, a bullock, and even a plough for her dowry. Then there was the expense of the wedding feast. As the *zamindar* knew, the feast had to include curried lamb and chicken, as well as rich dishes made with *paneer*, *chenna* cheese, saffron, and other expensive ingredients. Then there was a new *sari* for the bride, henna to decorate her hands, and even a few small pieces of gold jewelry.

The groom's family was downright greedy. "They are like vultures feeding on my carcass," Mr. Patke moaned. But what could a father do? Sunita was already past her fourteenth birthday. She *had* to be married quickly.

Mr. Patke glanced sadly at his three remaining daughters. Clearly, he was doing some depressing mental arithmetic. Mr. Ghosh gave him an extension on his loan.

The hut where the Garpure family lived seemed very crowded when Elizabeth ducked through the doorway. Until recently, the family's oldest sons, Ranajit and Sukumar, had been serving as soldiers in the province of Oudh. Oudh's native ruler, the *Nawab*, kept his own personal army. His soldiers were well paid, so the Garpure boys had been able to send money home. But the previous year, the Company had annexed the province, claiming that the *Nawab* was a depraved woman chaser, unfit to rule.

"The *Nawab* was not a very good ruler," Ranajit admitted, smiling. "We used to joke that his harem was bigger than his army. But that was no excuse for the Company to steal his land. And now the *Nawab*'s army no longer exists. All his soldiers were sent back to their families. There is no room here for Sukumar and me, but here we are anyway."

"My sons are hungry young men," Mr. Garpure added. "They have eaten the grain that I was planning to sell, so I cannot repay the *zamindar*'s kind loan."

That all seemed clear enough. Once again, Mr. Ghosh gave his tenants more time.

As they left the hut, he told Elizabeth, "The annexation of Oudh really was a disgrace. The Company simply trumped up an excuse for snatching the kingdom. Where is the English honor in that? And in fact, over the centuries many English rulers have consorted with women they were not married to—just like the *Nawab* of Oudh."

"Really?" Elizabeth said. This was not what she had been taught.

"Certainly. George the First brought two lady friends with him when he left Hanover to become King of England. One was short and fat, the other tall and skinny, and the English people called them the Elephant and the Maypole. So George's behavior was just a joke to his subjects! Certainly not something they thought he should lose his throne for. And well-behaved kings have always been thin on the ground. Everywhere. Even in England."

"But Queen Victoria—isn't she the height of domestic virtue?" Elizabeth protested.

"The Queen is merely the exception that proves the rule," Mr. Ghosh said.

When they reached home, Elizabeth saw Mrs. Ghosh and Pushpa look anxiously at Mr. Ghosh. He said nothing, but shook his head sadly. His wife and daughter were silent.

That night, Catherine wrote in her diary:

"This afternoon helped Mrs. G. make bright orange, super-sweet dessert called *jalebi*. Process too complicated even to remember, much less explain. *Sari*, alas, suffered badly. While working, Mrs. G. complained that Mr. G. is too kind. *'Now he will have to sell two fields because many peasants have not repaid his loans. Why does he not act like other **zamindars** and refuse credit? The **bania** would lend the peasants the money they need—and the **bania** know how to make people pay. Oh, yes, they know. But my husband does not know. If things go on like this, we will soon have no land left. Poor Mahin will end his life as a starving peasant.'* Mrs. G. was positively ranting. Not like usual gentle self.

Can see how decent *zamindars* might get squeezed between
the Company's demands and the peasants' needs. But would
Mr. G. want to survive if price of survival was to desert
peasants? As famous bard Shakespeare says in famous
tragedy, there is something rotten here. But what should be
done to fix it? Unfortunately, famous bard offers no answer.

Must go now, Diary, as Mrs. G. wants me to crush spices
for curry. Starvation may loom on horizon for Ghosh family,
but definitely not here yet. Mahin gobbled huge quantity of
jalebis. Will he turn orange?"

The next day, Elizabeth and Mr. Ghosh set off to visit
some peasants who lived outside the village. This
involved a long walk through the forest. Mr. Ghosh
offered to carry the ledger, but Elizabeth refused. He
looked so tired and sad. She didn't want to add to the
burdens he bore without complaining.

As they walked along the path between solid walls of
tangled greenery, Elizabeth kept wiping her face. This
outing is giving new meaning to the word trudge, she
told herself, pressing her lips together firmly. She was
determined to reclaim her reputation for toughness.
Never again would she give that nasty Pushpa an
opportunity to mock her.

Suddenly she heard a crashing in the underbrush. A
huge wild boar dashed into full view. Dark bristles
stood up along his backbone. His tusks gleamed. He
was so close that Elizabeth could see his black tongue
and sharp teeth as he charged straight at Mr. Ghosh.

Elizabeth had only a moment to think. Dropping the
ledger, she flung the entire weight of her body against

Mr. Ghosh as the boar dashed past. The force of the blow knocked the slender old man out of the boar's direct path. But one shining tusk ripped through the flesh of Mr. Ghosh's thigh, missing Elizabeth by inches. The beast galloped off into the forest. Terrified, Elizabeth scrambled to her feet and waited to see if he would turn and charge again. But he did not reappear.

Mr. Ghosh lay on the ground. A jagged red wound just below the bottom of his *dhoti* was spurting blood. Was there really so much blood in him? It seemed impossible. Elizabeth fought down the desire to flee from that horrible sight. She knew she had to stop the bleeding somehow.

Bandages, yes, bandages of course. With teeth and fingers, she began to tear strips off the edge of her *sari*. Then she wound them gently around Mr. Ghosh's leg, covering the gash. But the cloth immediately turned red, and the blood kept flowing. She felt panic rising in her throat.

"Tourniquet. Above the wound," Mr. Ghosh said in a weak voice. Then he fainted.

Elizabeth had no idea what a tourniquet was. Could it be a Hindi word? But she had to do something. Why had Mr. Ghosh said above the wound? Surely a bandage should be put *on* a wound, not above it? But she had already done that, and it wasn't helping at all.

Suddenly she remembered what she had learned about the circulation of the blood. If she closed off the blood vessels above the wound, the gash would stop bleeding.

A tourniquet must be something which could do that. And it must be something she could make out of what she had with her or Mr. Ghosh wouldn't have told her to make one. She had an idea.

Picking up a strip of cloth, Elizabeth wound it around Mr. Ghosh's thigh above the ugly gash. Then she twisted the loop again and again to tighten it. Below the strip of cloth—the tourniquet?—the wound abruptly stopped bleeding. Hands shaking violently, Elizabeth tied the tourniquet into place as best she could. Relief almost overpowered her.

But Mr. Ghosh remained motionless and the color did not come back to his face. Was he about to die?

Elizabeth's fear returned as she wondered what to do next. She had to get Mr. Ghosh back to the village. She couldn't possibly carry him, slim though he was. But how could she leave him? He might be attacked by any of the dangerous creatures that lived in the dark, throbbing jungle.

As she stood frozen with indecision, Mr. Ghosh's eyes opened. "*Go for help,*" he told her in a weak voice.

Elizabeth realized that he was right. This was his only chance. Summoning her scattered wits, she looked for the ledger she had dropped. She raised Mr. Ghosh's injured leg and slipped the big book under his foot. That way, his wound would be less likely to start bleeding again. Or so she hoped.

She tried to give Mr. Ghosh a reassuring smile, but managed only an anguished grimace. Then she turned and ran back towards the village. She tripped over a root and fell at full length. Her hands were scraped and filthy from her fall. Her *sari* started to unwind. But there was no time to think about that. She pressed on. As in a dream, she seemed to be making no progress whatever. Greenery hemmed her in on either side.

Close to collapse, Elizabeth burst out of the forest into the village. With her last ounce of strength, she sprinted into the Ghoshes' sitting room, gasping convulsively.

"Where is my father, Elizabeth?" Pushpa said, leaping to her feet. Her tone hovered between alarm and anger. "Is he in trouble? Have you deserted him?"

Elizabeth was unable to speak. Catherine ran for a glass of water and held it to her sister's lips. Elizabeth gulped it down. Mrs. Ghosh stood by, wringing her hands.

"Injured," Elizabeth gasped. "In the forest... On the path... Cannot walk... Send help... Bandages... Now."

Pushpa sprang into action. She sent servants to find a big pole and a stout tablecloth, which could be made into a hammock. She collected medicines and a bottle of water. She told her mother and Catherine to take care of Mahin. Then she and the servants set off at a run.

That night, Catherine wrote:

"Golly, Diary, what a day. Hours of waiting. Or so it seemed. Finally, Pushpa returned with Mr. G. in sling contraption. His face white as paneer. Mrs. G. plied him with strange Indian restoratives. As soon as Mr. G. able to talk, he called Elizabeth and thanked her. Sensation! Lizzie risked own life to rescue Mr. G. from gargantuan wild boar. Yes, Diary, *this* time woman saved man, not vice versa! Lizzie reacted to his praise by doing a fine imitation of

Fanny. 'Oh, it was nothing.' Never thought I would hear anything like that! Lizzie not usually one to hide light under bushel.

Mrs. G. started pressing jalebis on Lizzie. She even told Mahin, *'Don't eat those. We must save them for Madam Elizabeth.'* Will wonders never cease? Pushpa thanked Lizzie, but clearly wished she didn't have to. She would rather someone else had saved her father."

Exhausted, Elizabeth went early to bed. She soon slept, but her sleep was troubled. She was running through a dark, steamy forest. A tiger was chasing her. Papa appeared at her side and tried to distract the tiger by throwing handfuls of stamped, official papers in its face, but the tiger didn't even slow down. Elizabeth screamed as its claws sank into her flesh...

A hand shook her awake. What a relief. Surprised, Elizabeth saw Pushpa sitting on the edge of the bed that she shared with Catherine. Pointing to Catherine, who had not awakened, Pushpa put a finger to her lips. She patted Elizabeth's shoulder. Then she walked slowly out of the room.

CHAPTER EIGHTEEN: ARTISTIC EXPERIMENTS

Elizabeth recovered quickly. Mr. Ghosh did not. The gash became infected and he developed a low, persistant fever. Mrs. Ghosh wanted to help Pushpa care for him, but every time she tried to change the dressing on his wound, she fainted. The blood, the pus, the smell, the inflamed flesh — it was all too much for her.

Whenever this happened, Pushpa shouted to the servants, *"Throw some water on your mistress, for goodness sake. I can't leave my father. "* As soon as these measures revived Mrs. Ghosh, Pushpa would tell Catherine to dry the old lady off, take her into the kitchen, and keep her busy concocting something to tempt Mr. Ghosh's appetite.

And so it was that Elizabeth took Mrs. Ghosh's place as Pushpa's assistant. One of them stayed by Mr. Ghosh's side at all times. Despite Pushpa's protests, Elizabeth insisted on taking the night shift.

"You have to be awake during the day, Pushpa," she argued, "because of Mahin. Mahin needs to be able to at least see you and say a few words to you, even if you're busy nursing your father."

Night after night, by the dim glow of an oil lamp, Elizabeth wiped the sweat from Mr. Ghosh's face. He tossed restlessly, and sometimes he moaned quietly. When the light of dawn shone into the room, Elizabeth uncovered his wound. Forcing herself to inspect it carefully, she washed it with clean water and put on a fresh bandage. Then Pushpa arrived and between them, they changed Mr. Ghosh into clean *pyjamas*. After that, he seemed more comfortable, and Elizabeth could go to her room to sleep.

If praying weren't against my principles, Elizabeth told herself, I would pray for Mr. Ghosh. If he dies, I don't think I will be able to stand it. Pushpa won't either. And how could anybody in the village get along without him?

But Mr. Ghosh did not die. Gradually, the infection receded. His fever fell. A bit of color came back to his face, and he was able to sit up, propped on a pile of cushions. The wound began to heal. He no longer needed round the clock nursing.

Catherine wrote:

"August has arrived. The monsoon has too. We've actually been here almost three months. Mr. G. recovering, but still very weak. Will be bedridden for a long time. Mutiny/rebellion continues. Have had no news of Mama, Papa, James, or Ali. Too utterly horrible to think they may all be dead.

We visit Jane and Fanny whenever we can. Jane talks about crops and doesn't seem to care that she is in tatters. You don't believe that, Diary? Well, it's true. And almost every day, Fanny helps Mr. Simha do illegal things in the jungle. You don't believe that either? Well, it's also true.

Considered starting novel about how Jane and Fanny have changed, but am too agitated to work on large project. Besides, Diary, as you know, you are not big enough for me to write a novel in you. Must wait to start novel until we return home, if ever do. Have decided to write some poems instead. Poems lend themselves to cries from the heart.

Began a touching lament for lost love in style of popular poetess Mrs. Hemans, to be set in India. Wrote four lines:

'Tis Night, the temple gongs proclaim!
Not e'en a parrot whispers in the dell.
Alas! I come to view thy tomb, oh, James!
And bathe with tears the dust I loved too well.

Ugh. Apparently that's the sort of namby pamby stuff that comes out when you try to write like Mrs. Hemans. Of course, I'd be sad if James were killed, but I wouldn't drench his corpse in tears. I'm pretty sure that James is in love with Jane. And Jane is more utterly beautiful than ever these days, despite the rags she's wearing! Mama wouldn't be happy that Jane's so tanned, but the tan suits her.

Since the lost love poem didn't work out, decided to try a different subject: India. And a different style. Made a start:

What branches will grow
Out of this dusty soil,
When monsoon rains
Stir the dull roots?

Perhaps *you* think that doesn't sound like poetry, Diary, because I didn't use words like 'e'en' or 'alas.' And because it doesn't tinkle or rhyme. But *I* like it. It's grim, like the peasants' lives. Will see what Ali thinks if ever get to show it to him. What shall I call it? Perhaps 'The Sorrowful Land'?

But will have to work more on my poem later. Right now, must go wash *sari*, which suffered while making mud pies with Mahin. Monsoon to blame for that! There's a lot of tempting mud around."

Whenever Catherine wrote in her diary, Elizabeth glanced at her enviously. Now that she was no longer nursing Mr. Ghosh every waking moment, she didn't have enough to do. But she said nothing. It was her own fault for leaving her drawing materials behind.

On one of these occasions, Pushpa went into the bedroom she shared with Mahendra and returned with a box of paints, a sketchbook, and a *very* nice set of camel's hair brushes. It was almost as if she had read Elizabeth's thoughts.

"I brought these with me from my former life, Lizzie," she said, dumping them on the table in front of Elizabeth. "While he still loved me, Lieutenant Jennings wanted me to be accomplished, like an English lady, so he had me taking drawing lessons. I hate the sight of these things now. I was saving them for Mahin. But who knows if he will ever want them? You may as well take them."

A smile of delight added luster to Elizabeth's dark eyes as she thanked Pushpa.

"I love the paintings you have on your walls, Pushpa. Rajput miniatures, they're called — isn't that right? All those little figures in their tiny, perfect houses are fantastic. Not to mention the brilliant colors. Scarlet, gold, mauve, midnight blue. I'm going to try making my own Rajput style paintings."

"Maybe I would have enjoyed painting more if I'd done that too," Pushpa said.

"Why didn't you, then?" asked Elizabeth.

"Well, my teacher was English. When I started to paint a temple, he'd tell me, 'A religious building shouldn't look like a merry go round. So you must tone down the colors. And you can just leave out those absurd blue cows.' I argued with him. I told him that since our temples really are brightly colored, they should be painted that way."

"That sounds perfectly reasonable to me," Elizabeth said. She could never keep silent when painting was being discussed.

"To me too. But my teacher would just repeat what I had questioned. 'No,' he'd say, 'A religious building must evoke the sacred. And that must be done by using soft, dignified colors, as well as *chiaroscuro* and perspective.' There was no way I could win the argument. So I gave up painting when my husband deserted me. Anyway, I wasn't much good at it."

"Well, I know all about *chiaroscuro*," Elizabeth said. "It just means using contrasts between light and dark to give a sense of depth. Perspective also gives a sense of depth. Your teacher probably thought those techniques were suited to sacred subjects, since religious truth is supposed to be the deepest thing there is."

"Perhaps he did."

"But different techniques might work better sometimes," Elizabeth continued. "Though lots of people think religion is deeply true, I don't agree. I think people turn to religion because it offers them hope for a brighter future. You might get that optimism into a religious picture by using bright colors."

"Indian paintings actually do something along those lines," Pushpa said, sounding surprised. "They link the divine to a sense of bursting life, and even to a naughty sense of fun. They show the god Krishna spying on beautiful maidens swimming in the nude — and getting into other mischief of the same sort."

"Really?" Elizabeth asked, "I didn't know that. But I do know that Rajput paintings really give you the feel of India. There are no shadows in them. Everything is bathed in a clear light, like the light of the Indian sun at midday."

"Yes," Pushpa said in the bitter tone she so often used, "I think so too. But the English are always ready to abuse our ways. They call our art primitive and our religion barbaric, even though our culture is far older than theirs. Our ancestors had already written the Ramayana while yours were running around the forest painted blue and whacking one another with clubs."

Elizabeth did not answer. She wasn't about to get into an argument with someone who had just given her a box of paints.

CHAPTER NINETEEN: A VIOLENT EVENT

August passed slowly. Mr. Ghosh remained in bed. The monsoon deluged the village with solid walls of water. Every once in a while, it stopped abruptly, and the sun shone brilliantly from a pure blue sky.

The Ghoshes heard via the 'jungle telegraph' that the English force was still camped on the ridge overlooking Delhi, falling prey to cholera and other diseases. The mutineers gathered in Delhi had attacked this force many times, but without success. At various stations in the north of India, more regiments of *sepoys* were mutinying every few days.

But the Company had three armies, and only its Bengal army was involved in the mutiny. The Madras army and the Bombay army were still loyal to the Company. Reinforcements from these armies might arrive at any time to help the outnumbered English soldiers at Delhi. Though it was by no means clear when the conflict was going to end, it was starting to seem that the English would eventually win it. The mutiny had taken them by surprise, but once they mobilized their resources, they would outnumber and outgun the rebels. And unlike the rebels, they had the money to pay their soldiers indefinitely.

The Ghoshes heard nothing about the fate of Shivapur. But upsetting news of a different sort did reach them. Small bands of rebels were roaming through the countryside killing every foreigner they could find. And several of these murderous bands were approaching Murarmau. The fury of the uprising was not yet spent.

Considering what she now knew about the Company's *raj*, Elizabeth was not surprised.

There seemed to be nothing to do except what they were already doing. They waited, tensely, and they did not have long to wait.

One morning in September when the monsoon was taking a breather, four strange young men, armed with swords and wearing tattered *sepoy* uniforms, walked into the Ghoshes' house, demanding food. Three of them looked ordinary enough, but the fourth was a gigantic Sikh, with a bushy, black beard. Frightened, Mrs. Ghosh served them a huge meal. Catherine and Elizabeth moved about quietly in the background, trying to look Indian.

The strangers left the house as soon as they finished eating. They had barely looked at anyone. Perhaps they had chosen the biggest house in the village to visit simply because they thought they'd get some good food there? But if they didn't suspect the Ghoshes of hiding foreigners, why had they come to the village at all? Did they suspect another family? Or were they just passing through?

Running to the doorway, Pushpa, Catherine, and Elizabeth saw the men walking across the marketplace, straight towards the Simhas' hut, which was set apart from its neighbors.

"Oh, no," Catherine gasped. "Do you suppose someone told them that two fair-haired girls are living there?"

"So much for the idea of hiding you girls in plain sight," Pushpa said sadly. "I should have known that even one informer could ruin that plan. Why did I count on the villagers' loyalty? Why was I so sure they would listen to my father when he asked them to help you? Didn't my husband show me how treacherous people can be? How ungrateful? What a fool I am!"

"I don't think it was one of the villagers," Elizabeth said. "It must have been a stranger who saw Fanny or Jane as he passed through the village. They keep forgetting to pull up their *dupattas*, and when their heads are uncovered they stick out like two sore thumbs. A treacherous peasant would have told the rebels that Catherine and I were hiding at your house. But those four *sepoys* don't know that. They didn't even look at us."

"Yes, that makes sense. Thank Lord Shiva, the peasants must still be on my father's side. Heaven knows he deserves it. It would be terrible if they betrayed him after all he's done for them. We must act quickly. Lizzie, you know where the Garpures live. Run and tell Ranajit and Sukumar what has happened. They must take their swords and go to the Simhas' house. Warn them not to attract attention on the way."

Elizabeth did as she was told.

Pushpa raced from the room and returned with a polished wooden box. It held an up-to-date pistol.

"My father keeps this gun loaded. There is always danger from *dacoits*."

Pushpa and Catherine rushed outside. They could see the four strangers ahead of them, sauntering slowly, as even energetic young men will after a heavy meal washed down by many cups of *lassi*.

Hiding the pistol under her *sari*, Pushpa trailed behind the strangers, keeping her distance. Catherine stayed by Pushpa's side.

Soon Catherine saw Elizabeth walking toward the Simhas' hut from the opposite direction. Her manner was exaggeratedly casual. With her were Ranajit and Sukumar Garpure, sauntering along as if they hadn't a care in the world. Each of them was holding something behind his back. Catherine devoutly hoped it was a sword.

Pushpa stared at the strangers ahead of her. She lifted her revolver and took careful aim at the Sikh. Catherine was horrified. Was Pushpa really going to shoot him in the back? Could anything be more brutal, more uncivilized? But even as Catherine stood paralyzed, Pushpa lowered the gun.

"No, I cannot," she muttered. *"They are my countrymen."* A look of agony appeared on her beautiful face.

The strangers had nearly reached the Simhas' hut, when Jane suddenly appeared in the doorway, carrying a deep basket. She was leaving for her work in the fields. Her head was bare, and her bright hair gleamed in the hot sunlight.

One of the strangers lunged towards Jane, making a grab for her *sari*. Reflexively, Jane lifted the empty basket and popped it over his head and shoulders. The young man dropped his sword. He staggered from side to side, trying to disentangle himself from the basket.

Seeing three more strangers in *sepoy* uniforms

approaching, Jane realized what was happening. She felt sure she was about to die.

But just as the first stranger managed to wrench the basket off his head, Sukumar ran up and struck the man a stunning blow with the flat of his sword. As the man fell to the ground, Sukumar finished him off with a single thrust. Looking quite unruffled, Sukumar turned toward the other three strangers.

Inside, the hut, Fanny had also realized what was going on. She was urging the family to flee.

"They are here to kill us, not you," she said. "If you run now and I stay here, they will not chase you."

"No, Madam Fanny," Mr. Simha protested, "I must stand my ground. I would be no better than a woman, if I left you to die."

Mrs. Simha motioned angrily toward her husband. "Better a live dog than a dead lion, you fool! Can you think of nothing but your precious manhood?"

Grabbing Mr. Simha's arm, she pulled him out of the hut. Kasthuri followed, carrying Krishna. They disappeared into the forest.

From the doorway, Fanny saw two strange men battling with Ranajit and Sukumar Garpure. A third man lay motionless on the ground, a basket near his head. For a moment, Fanny thought he was sleeping. He looked quite relaxed. But then she noticed the red stain on his chest.

From the sidelines, Catherine was also watching in growing horror. Ranajit and one of the strangers were fighting each other with swords. It was just like a play.

Shakespeare, or perhaps Marlowe?

The stranger was getting the upper hand. He slashed Ranajit's arm and lunged forward. Just in time, Catherine took a flying leap and landed on the stranger's back. She clung to him with all her strength. As the man danced about trying to shake Catherine off, Ranajit scrambled out of the way.

The stranger looked over his shoulder and realized that the attacker clinging to his back was a woman. A look of disbelief came over his face, as he tried to escape from her grip.

Fanny wanted to go to Catherine's aid, but her feet refused to move. She shrank back against the wall of the hut.

Ranajit clutched at his wounded arm. He shook his head from side to side. Where was he? What was happening? As his vision cleared, he saw the stranger trying to scrape Catherine off his back against a mango tree. Running straight at the man, Ranajit spitted him on his sword. As the man fell, Catherine dropped to the ground with a cry of pain.

Ranajit saw that Catherine was bleeding. His sword had gone right through the man's body like a knife through ghee—and its point had pierced Catherine's chest. As he bent over Catherine, Ranajit prayed to every god he could think of that the wound was not serious. He barely knew this girl, but he didn't want to be guilty of killing her, even accidentally.

Jane saw none of this. Her eyes were fixed on the *sepoy* Sukumar had just killed. She was horrified at what

Sukumar had done.

But Sukumar felt no such horror. His soldierly training had kicked in. Turning away from the body of his victim, he had already attacked the third stranger. As Jane watched, he knocked the sword from the stranger's hand, but lost his grip on his own weapon in the process. Kicking both swords out of the way, Sukumar wrestled the man to the ground.

Jane picked up one of the swords. The glittering weapon shook in her hand as she looked at the tangle of men at her feet. How could she be sure that she wouldn't wound the wrong man if she attacked? She jumped backward as they rolled towards her.

Jane realized that no one was going to help her. She remembered that Sukumar had just saved her life. She *had* to help him. And she had to do it *now*.

"Sukumar, let him go. Roll out of the way," she said urgently. Sukumar did as he was told. Raising the sword high, Jane forced herself to strike. Then she flung the weapon away with all her strength. The third **sepoy** died quickly.

Meanwhile Pushpa had launched herself at the big Sikh, pistol in hand. She motioned Elizabeth to help her. As Elizabeth grabbed his arm, Pushpa tried hit him with the pistol butt. She didn't want to shoot him if she could avoid it. But the joint efforts of the two slim girls didn't even slow the huge man down.

He looked at them and smiled contemptuously. With an almost relaxed sweep of the arm, he flung Pushpa away. Staggering, she saw him grab Elizabeth by the throat. Did he think he could finish Elizabeth off and then kill her? But he hadn't seen that she was armed.

Pushpa jumped to her feet and aimed her gun. This time she did not hesitate. The Sikh fell, shot through the head. Freed from his grip, Elizabeth gasped for air. Pushpa dropped the gun.

All four strangers lay lifeless on the ground.

Fanny ran to Catherine. Pushing aside the bloody *sari*, she was relieved to see that her sister's wound was not at all serious. With the end of her own *sari*, Fanny staunched the bleeding. Catherine opened her eyes.

"I wasn't unconscious," she said, "but I couldn't bear to watch the rest of you battling for our lives while I was hors de combat. Isn't 'hors de combat' an utterly marvelous phrase? It's French. It sounds so much better than 'unable to fight.'"

Ranajit looked as if he thought Catherine had gone insane. What on earth was she talking about? But Fanny knew her sister. Even on her deathbed, Catherine would be searching for the best phrase to describe the experience.

"You're still *hors de combat*, Catherine," Fanny said in English. "Don't even think about getting up."

Elizabeth was trying to come to terms with what had happened. It had been so sudden. So violent. Had they really killed *all* of the strangers? They had been seven against four, counting Ranajit and Sukumar. That was hardly fair. And yet, what else could they have done? It wasn't as if they'd been playing cricket. Rules of fair play simply didn't apply. But even so...

She saw that Ranajit and Sukumar looked very sad. Though they were used to killing, they hadn't wanted to kill other Indians. Their sympathies were with the mutineers. They had only defended the May girls because Mr. Ghosh had said that if rebels came to Murarumau, the villagers couldn't stand by and let innocent blood be shed.

Of course, Mr. Ghosh had been hoping that there would be no bloodshed at all, that things would work out for the best. But things hadn't worked out that way. They seldom did, Elizabeth thought.

Jane's ragged *sari* was spattered with blood. Hands covering her face, she sobbed uncontrollably. She would never be able to forget the face of the man she had killed. He was so young... She struggled for calm.

Sukumar took charge.

"We must bury the bodies. If other *sepoys* come looking for these men, we will say that we have never seen them. We will tell everyone in the village to say the same."

He went into the Simhas' hut to look for a shovel.

"Yes, we must hide the bodies," Pushpa said in a shaky voice. "But that will solve only part of our problem. The strangers knew exactly where Fanny and Jane were living. So other rebels probably know this as well. When they realize that their friends have disappeared, they will come to the village to find the foreigners. You girls must leave Murarmau. You are not safe here."

Pushpa really is worried about us, Elizabeth thought. She killed the Sikh to save me and not just to obey her father.

As if she could read Elizabeth's mind, Pushpa snapped, "Don't think this changes anything, Elizabeth. I still hate the English. And I still don't want Mahin to grow up in a country ruled by foreigners."

"That goes without saying," Elizabeth answered. But she was unable to suppress a smile. "Now we must talk to your father. He will know what to do."

"Jane must go with you," Fanny said. "It is dangerous for her to stay at the Simhas' a minute longer, since the *sepoys* knew that she was hiding there. She will be safest with Mr. Ghosh."

"You must come with us too," Catherine said.

"No, I must go to the forest to find the Simhas and tell them to return. I'm sure that they will be in the clearing where Mr. Simha and I make charcoal. Though there's no path, I've been there so often that I think I can find it by myself."

"Oh, Fanny," Catherine moaned, "It's not safe for you to go crashing around in the underbrush all by yourself. There are snakes. And leeches. And think of the wild boar that almost killed Mr. Ghosh."

"Yes," Jane said, suppressing her sobs, "And suppose more rebels come looking for us? You might stumble on them before you find the Simhas, and then..."

"No, this is my duty, Fanny said firmly. "I am the only one who knows where to find the Simhas. And we owe them so much." Squaring her small shoulders, she walked straight into the jungle before anyone could stop her.

Elizabeth watched her go with mixed feelings. Fanny was probably wishing that Papa could see her as she set off on her dangerous mission. Though she had changed a lot, Fanny was Fanny still.

Leaving Ranajit and Sukumar to bury the bodies, Pushpa and the three May sisters made their way back to the Ghoshes' house. Jane and Elizabeth supported Catherine between them. A flock of crows squawked overhead. Gray clouds had gathered, and a few big drops of rain began to fall. The monsoon was starting up again.

CHAPTER TWENTY: A SIMPLE PLAN

Mr. Ghosh agreed that the girls had to leave the village immediately.

"I have not been lying here all these weeks without thinking," he said, with his usual sweet smile. "I have a plan ready, and the time has come to use it. The monsoon rains have raised the level of our small river. It is navigable only at this time of year. You will escape by boat. You will float downstream."

"But we don't have a boat," Catherine objected. "You don't have one either, do you? And where does the river go? Floating down it might just take us deeper into danger."

"Don't be silly, Catherine," Elizabeth said irritably, "Don't you know Mr. Ghosh by now? Of course he has thought of all that."

"Of course he has," Pushpa said. "And he's thought of less obvious things, too."

"Well, yes, I have," Mr. Ghosh said calmly. "I own a boat, which I can use only during the monsoon. I keep it in the jungle during the dry season. All we need to do now is to launch it. You will be in some danger, because the first stretch of the river runs through rebel territory. But then the river passes into an area that's now in English hands. You can float down that stretch quite safely."

"Oh, Father," Pushpa cried, "I see what you're thinking. The river goes through Arjunabad, where Devender lives. The girls can leave the boat there and the boatwallah can row it back. Devender can take them in his cart to Meerut. Meerut has been under the Company's control since the rebels left it for Delhi right after the mutiny."

"What a wonderful plan," Jane said, brightening up a bit. "With luck we will find Papa and Mama in Meerut."

She did not add that she hoped to find Lieutenant Palliser there as well.

"Mr. Ghosh," Elizabeth said, "no words can say how much we owe you. You are the... simply the... " She bit her lip and fell silent.

"My father knows how you feel about him, Lizzie," Pushpa said quietly. "No words are needed."

A few moments passed. Suddenly, Elizabeth threw her arms around Pushpa and buried her face in Pushpa's neck.

Mahendra stared for a moment and then ran to them, shouting, "*In – let me in. I want to go in the hug!*"

Mahendra pushed himself under his mother's arm, and she and Elizabeth squeezed him hard between their bodies. Everyone was laughing.

But the sisters had to get ready for their journey.

Under a stormy sky, Jane walked across the village to see if Fanny had brought the Simhas back from the forest. To her relief, she found them all gathered in the hut. Fanny's arms were covered with scratches, but she looked almost happy.

Mission accomplished, Jane thought. Accomplishing an unpleasant mission always cheered Fanny up.

Jane explained Mr. Ghosh's plan. Since there was nothing for Jane and Fanny to pack, it was time to say good-bye.

Jane took Mrs. Simha's hands. Between her horror at the violence she'd taken part in and her sorrow at leaving the Simhas, she was close to breaking down, but Mrs. Simha was having none of that.

"You have become an excellent farmer, Madam Jane," she said briskly, "but I am afraid you will need many weeks, and perhaps the aid of a higher power as well, to regain the white skin and soft hands you had when you came to us. I hope this will not harm your chances of making a good marriage when you return to your people."

"Well, I wouldn't want to marry anyone who cared what color my skin was," Jane snapped. Mrs. Simha smiled. She had been hoping to distract Jane from her grief.

But it was not possible to distract Fanny. She was glad that the Simhas would have fewer mouths to feed now, but how could Mr. Simha possibly get along without her help? The thought of him building wooden igloos all by himself in the depths of the jungle was heartrending. And that wasn't the worst of it. When the Company regained control of Murarmau, the Simhas would have to stay out of the forest. Krishna might go hungry.

Taking the little boy on her lap, Fanny vowed that she would come back some day to help the Simhas. She wouldn't forget what they had done for her. She could never be so ungrateful as that.

Jane and Fanny stooped through the low doorway of the hut and walked toward the Ghoshes' house. They found Catherine and Elizabeth waiting outside. In a big bundle, Elizabeth was carrying the dresses the sisters had been wearing when they came to the village. Catherine was carrying her notebook and Elizabeth's drawing supplies.

The *boatwallah*, Avilash, had collected the food and water they would need on the journey. He motioned to Jane and Fanny to help him carry it.

"I hate farewells," Elizabeth said in English. "They're horribly soppy. The Ghoshes know that we know how much we owe them. And we know that they know that we know. And they know—well, you get the idea. Since there's really no point in going over it again and again, we said good-bye to them for you."

"Looking at it from that angle, one could hardly disagree," Jane said with a wan smile. "So the only thing to do now is to get the dangerous part of the journey over with as quickly as possible."

With a strong, sure movement that surprised Elizabeth, Jane lifted a heavy jar of water and balanced it on her head. They followed Avilash towards the river.

The group walked upstream on a narrow path. Rain fell softly. A brilliant green parrot darted across the river in front of them and disappeared into the trees. Fanny wondered if crocodiles were lurking in the muddy water. No one had mentioned crocodiles during her stay in the village, but you could never be sure. There was a suspicious looking ripple near the opposite bank. Fanny shuddered and looked away.

Avilash turned off the path and pushed his way into the foliage. Mr. Ghosh's boat was sitting on a wheeled contraption used for rolling it to the edge of the river. The boat reminded Catherine of the fishing dorys she had seen in England, though it was smaller and flatter. Catherine didn't think it looked seaworthy, but probably it was riverworthy enough. Pressing her hand to her injured midriff, she smiled at the word she had invented.

Once the boat was loaded, the girls and Avilash climbed carefully in. Avilash pushed off into the sluggish current and took charge of the rudder. The wide, shallow river was tricky to navigate, but he knew it well. He would be able to keep them away from the treacherous quicksands that had swallowed many a stranded boat, passengers and all.

Though drifting with the current would eventually get them where they wanted to go, Jane decided to speed things up by rowing. After all, they had to pass through rebel territory before reaching the British-held area. It made sense to finish this part of the trip as fast as they could. Jane certainly wasn't eager to meet any more mutineers. One murder was one too many, she reflected sadly. She grabbed the oars, fitted them into the oarlocks, and began rowing vigorously.

Elizabeth saw what her sister had in mind.

"Let me know when you get tired, Jane," she said, "and I'll take a spell at the oars. Catherine shouldn't row because her cut might open up and start bleeding again, and Fanny can't row because she's too small. So you and I will have to take turns."

"Goodness, Elizabeth," Jane said with sisterly malice, "you're starting to sound as selfless as Fanny. You'd better watch it."

"I don't sound like Fanny at all," Elizabeth retorted. "The person I sound like is Mr. Ghosh. I'm solving practical problems to help us *all* survive—just the way he does."

"No," Jane said, resting on her oars, "you used to say that you wanted to put *yourself* first. Now you say you're acting for the good of the whole group. You really are more like Fanny than you used to be."

Elizabeth grimaced, but said nothing.

"Well, one thing's for sure, Lizzie," Catherine added. "You'll be making nasty remarks about Fanny until the end of time. The more things change the more they remain the same, as someone or other put it."

The girls fell silent. Though they were all nervous about the possibility of meeting more rebels, the trip downriver proved surprisingly enjoyable. Elizabeth took out the sketchbook Pushpa had given her and began to draw the foliage on the banks.

Feathery grasses with downy white seeds grew so thickly that in places it looked as if the ground was covered with snow. Behind the grasses towered tall, dark trees. In their branches, families of cheeky gray monkeys went about their business undisturbed. Fanny was enchanted by the tiny, bright-eyed babies who clung so tightly to their mothers' backs. The biggest male monkeys with their superbly dignified expressions reminded her of something.

"Do you think we will find Papa in Meerut?" she asked Catherine.

"I'd like to say yes, Fanny, but I really can't. We may find that all of our friends are alive in Meerut, or it might turn out that they have all been killed. Maybe Devender will have some news when we get to Arjunabad."

"I certainly hope to find Lieutenant Palliser alive," Jane said boldly.

"But not James Keats?" Catherine asked.

"Oh, James too, of course. But James is not likely to have been in much danger. Even if there was fighting in Malior, and we don't know if there was, the English wouldn't have harmed him because he's English."

"But what about the rebels?" Fanny said anxiously.

"The rebels wouldn't harm him because he works for an Indian ruler. Then too, James isn't very heroic. *I've* actually killed a man with my own hands. Admittedly, it's not something I'd like to do every day before breakfast. Indeed, though I'm trying to joke about it, it made me feel awful and it still does."

"I don't think you should even *try* to joke about it," Fanny interrupted.

"Why not? It can't harm the poor man I killed. He's dead, and he'll stay dead whether I laugh or cry. But I doubt James could do what I did under any circumstances. Lieutenant Palliser not only can, but has, many times."

"James is no coward," Catherine said angrily. "If he

stays out of the fighting it won't be to save his skin. It will be because his sympathies are divided. My sympathies are divided too. I learned a lot about the Company's *raj* while we were in Murarmau, and nothing I learned made me think it's good for India."

"Yes, I feel that way as well," Jane said. "I suppose all of us have become 'white Indians' like James. Though maybe in a different way. Maybe Lieutenant Palliser and I won't agree about anything when we meet again — if we ever do."

Catherine heart sank.

"I'm getting awfully tired of that monotonous greenness," she said, gazing into the trees.

CHAPTER TWENTY-ONE: ARJUNABAD

The stretch of river down which they were now floating was wide and deep.

"I will show Madam Fanny how to steer," Avilash said. "When the moon rises, she can take over and I will get some sleep. We are lucky that it has stopped raining.

"And you and I can row all night if we do it in shifts," Elizabeth said to Jane.

The night passed slowly and uneventfully. In the dim light of a crescent moon, Elizabeth struggled to stay awake. The temptation to stop rowing, put her head on her knees, and close her eyes was almost irresistible. But she resisted it and kept rowing. She knew that their safety might depend on her efforts.

Elizabeth could see Fanny sitting motionless and upright, carefully guiding the rudder. She was softly humming a hymn, *"New Every Morning is the Love."*

Catherine, who had been sleeping in the bottom of the boat, suddenly woke up. She lay still for a few moments, then raised her head.

"Yes, Fanny, it is a new morning," she said. "I don't usually get to see the dawn. I'm not much of an early riser. But today I will. I wonder if it's really rosy fingered, like it says in *The Iliad*."

She gazed intently eastward.

"No, it's not rosy at all," she said in disappointed tones after a few minutes, "The sky is as gray as Mr. Beaglehole's hair. Utterly unrosy, in fact."

"Do you think it's going to start pouring on us?" Elizabeth asked Avilash, looking anxiously at the sky. Suppose they had to bail as well as row? She was getting pretty tired.

"It may rain," he answered, "but perhaps it will not, for the monsoon season is ending. And even if it rains, there is nothing to worry about. We are now in British held territory, and around that big bend in front of us is the city of Arjunabad. We will be there in less time than it takes to cook a *chapatti*. This has been a fortunate journey, praise the Lord Krishna for that."

"Will we be able to find Devender's house? Fanny said.

"Certainly. Devender comes from Murarmau, and we always visit him when we come to the city. Now let us look for a good place to beach the boat."

After tying up the boat, Avilash and the sisters picked their way amid piles of rubbish and dung, saffron robed holy men holding out their begging bowls, and tiny shops crammed with bright bolts of cloth and bags of colorful spices.

The girls were surprised to find themselves inhaling the mingled smells with pleasure. Like Shivapur, Arjunabad was a town, and after the quiet of tiny Murarmau, it seemed very much like home. Passersby stared curiously at Jane and Fanny. Blondes wearing tattered *saris* were not an everyday sight. Jane enjoyed the attention. Fanny pulled her *dupatta* over her face. She was relieved when they reached Devender's small hut.

Devender was inside, eating his *chota hazri*. He

jumped to his feet.

"You're alive!" he cried. "Alive, by Durga! We heard that *sepoys* were on the way to Murarmau to kill you. It was too late to do anything. We thought you would certainly die."

"Well, actually we killed the *sepoys*," Jane said. "All of them. It was them or us."

"And we buried their bodies in secret, so you mustn't say anything about it." Elizabeth said prudently. "News seems to spread so fast. If other rebels find out what happened to their friends, they will go to the village to take revenge. Mr. Ghosh and Pushpa — oh, and the other villagers too — would be in danger."

"But Devender," Fanny interrupted, "You must tell us everything you know. Papa and Mama? Our friends from Shivapur? Where are they? And where is Komal?"

"Komal has gone to help your parents. They managed to reach Meerut before the rebellion spread, even though the local peasants did not give your father the help he expected from them. In fact, they tried to kill him. His feelings were badly hurt. But he and your mother did get away, and they have been in Meerut ever since. Your father recovered from his sickness. But — "

"Oh, great Lord God," Fanny said in English, falling to her knees and raising her clasped hands in prayer. "I thank Thee for preserving *all* our friends from harm." Turning to her sisters she added triumphantly, "You see? It's just as I've always told you. God moves in a mysterious way His wonders to perform."

The other girls looked uneasy.

"But what, Devender? What were you going to say?" Catherine asked anxiously.

"But many of the English in Shivapur were killed the day Komal and I helped you to flee. Some escaped, but most were cut down as they tried to run away. They died in the streets, in the Residency. Women and children as well as men. Their bodies were everywhere. And Shivapur is still in rebel hands."

God moves in a mysterious way indeed, Elizabeth thought sourly, but she said nothing. It didn't seem like the right moment to undermine Fanny's faith.

"What happened to the Barnfathers, to the Browns?" Jane asked.

"I do not know," Devender said. "But you can soon find out. The territory between Arjunabad and Meerut is under the Company's control now, so as soon as you have eaten something, I can take you to Meerut in my cart. Komal told your parents where you were hiding, but of course they have been very worried. I do not know if they heard about the *sepoys* who went to kill you. We can only hope they did not."

Devender cooked up some fresh, hot *chappattis*, but the girls were too nervous to eat much. Avilash devoured his portion and left for the return trip to Murarmau.

An hour later, the sisters were sitting in Devender's cart wearing the European clothes in which they had fled from Shivapur, ready to leave for Meerut. Jane felt uncomfortable in her shabby dress. It seemed to fit very differently from the way it used to. The short sleeves pinched her strong arms. She must look a perfect fright, and soon she might be seeing Lieutenant Palliser again. Oh, dear.

Since they were getting an early start, they would be able to reach Meerut the same day.

The May girls had never been to Arjunabad, and the road from there to Meerut was completely unfamiliar to them. Fall crops of maize, sorghum, and sesame seed had been planted in the fields by the roadside, but the fields looked very unhealthy. Their colors tended toward a dusty greenish gray. The area was bare of people.

"The peasants who should be hoeing the crops are utterly not there," Catherine said in surprise, "Where can they all have gone?"

"*See for yourself,*" Devender said sadly, waving his hand in a comprehensive gesture. Catherine looked more closely at the fields, and saw that they had been trampled down in many places. The patches were awfully weedy. Raising her eyes, she saw the remains of a small village ahead of them.

"That village looks like it's been burned to the ground," she exclaimed in horror.

"Yes, that's right. After the mutiny, General John Nicholson formed a small army that he called the Moveable Column. That sounds harmless enough, but its purpose was to rush around the rebel held areas to terrorize the peasants into submission, and —"

"John Nicholson?" Fanny broke in, "I've heard of him

from Papa. Papa doesn't like him at all. Papa said Nicholson doesn't know fear, but he doesn't know compassion either. And Papa also said that Nicholson hates Indians. Papa thinks it is dangerous to trust such men with power."

"It certainly is," Devender said. "When he was a district commissioner, Nicholson cut off the head of a *dacoit* and kept it on his desk as a souvenir. That was his idea of humor. You can imagine what he must be like when he's feeling serious!"

There was a moment of silence while everyone considered Devender's suggestion.

"After the rebellion broke out," Devender continued, "Nicholson said that he would torture any mutineer he caught—and that he'd do it with a clear conscience! But of course, as soon as the Company feared for its *raj*, it gave this cruel man command of an army. On the way to join the attack on Delhi, Nicholson burned every village he passed. He stopped killing the men he captured by blowing them to pieces from the mouths of cannon only because he'd decided it was a waste of powder. And he..."

"Please stop," Fanny moaned, "I can't bear any more."

Catherine thought that Devender had a lot more he wanted to say, but he didn't say it. It was nice of him to consider Fanny's feelings. Catherine felt utterly sick. Would there be no end to this murder? This hatred?

"Do you hate Indians, Jane?" she asked in English. "You killed one, after all. Of course, I have to admit that I helped kill another."

"No, I don't," Jane said slowly, "I keep telling myself that I only killed in self-defense, but I'd be a lot happier if we could have saved ourselves without killing anyone. And I'm not going to forget that the Simhas and the Ghoshes are Indians too."

"Yes," Elizabeth added, "and Mr. Ghosh is the best man I've ever known. He —"

"Oh, Lizzie, please—that's enough about Mr. Ghosh," Catherine said, rolling her eyes.

Tearing her gaze away from the ruined village, Fanny stared straight ahead, willing Meerut to come into view. Only when she was once again with her parents, especially Papa, would she feel safe. He would think for her, and she would have nothing to do but obey him. Or would she? She had done a lot of things in Murarmau that Papa would never have approved, much less ordered. So it was possible that she'd want to disobey him in future. What a disquieting thought.

The sun was setting when Devender's cart rattled into the civil lines of Meerut. Some of the bungalows had been burned, but others were still standing. Indian servants and a few Europeans moved about the wide, straight streets, but the sisters saw no one they knew.

The monsoon was ending, and there was a hint of coolness in the air. A flock of swallows darted about overhead, feasting on invisible midges. The sky, a lovely, velvety blue, was growing blacker every moment. It was the sixteenth of September.

CHAPTER TWENTY-TWO: REUNION

Devender's cart rattled to a stop in front of the very same bungalow where James Keats had been sleeping when the mutiny began. The *dak* bungalow. Komal appeared in the doorway, holding a lamp. When she saw Devender and the girls, she gave a cry of delight and then swiftly put a finger to her lips.

"Wait here, my daughters," she said, "I must tell your mother gently that you have come, lest the shock of seeing you be too much for her. She has been very worried, even hysterical at times. Your father has often told her sternly to keep calm, but of course that only upset her the more. I will call you in just a moment."

"Poor Mama," Catherine said to her sisters, "I can imagine what it's been like for her, left to Papa's tender mercies. He thinks women are utterly weak by nature, but when he gets annoyed with Mama's hysterics, he turns around and orders her to be strong. How illogical men are! "

Inside the bungalow, Mrs. May was sitting in an armchair with a mug of steaming masala tea, trying to read a novel.

Komal squatted down next to her.

"*Memsahib*, I am bringing good news," she said in English, "Something you have been long wishing now happening. Daughters are well. Daughters are arriving. In fact, daughters are here."

Komal went to the door and beckoned the girls to enter. Mrs. May jumped to her feet and began to cry as four pairs of arms encircled her.

The sisters all talked at once, each one telling a part of their story. None of them realized that their mother wasn't taking any of it in. Mrs. May kept squeezing them one after another, as if to assure herself that all of them were really there.

Hearing the hubbub, Mr. May walked in from the next room. Despite his small stature, or perhaps because of it, his posture was always very upright.

Fanny ran straight into his arms.

"My little Fanny," he cried, "Do I really see my little Fanny?"

For a moment, his face glowed with relief. Then he resumed his usual lofty expression.

Hugs and kisses finally over with, the family sat down to talk. The girls repeated their story. Mrs. May listened with horror.

"A python, a cobra, a wild boar?" she moaned, "Floating downriver through rebel territory all by yourselves? Jane killing a man with her own hands? My sweet little girls, how is it even possible?"

"Well, we didn't actually travel to Arjunabad all by ourselves," Elizabeth pointed out, "Avilash the boatwallah was with us, and he knows the river."

"Oh, an Indian servant..." Mrs. May said, recovering her ordinary tone of voice, "That hardly counts. And to think that you were travelling with him unchaperoned. I hope none of our friends get to hear of this."

"Well, I see we're back in British India again,"

Catherine said. "Even a bunch of near death experiences and a few murders can't make Mama forget the proprieties."

"Your mother's concern with decorum is quite appropriate," Mr. May reproved her. "And I am not completely happy that my little women should have forgotten this, even under unusual circumstances. We must always remember that —"

Elizabeth interrupted him impatiently.

"Oh, heavens, Papa, let's *not* remember that sort of thing just now. Do tell us what's happened to all our friends. Ali? James? The Browns? We have had no news at all."

Mr. May looked a bit affronted.

"By the time your mother and I got to Meerut," he said, "a few refuges from Shivapur were already here. There weren't many of them. Mrs. Brown and the Barnfathers died in Shivapur, but Lieutenant Palliser helped Reverend Brown and Susan escape. They wandered through the jungle for days. They were set upon by armed *gujars* out for plunder. Susan's earrings were literally ripped from her bleeding ears. By the end, they were starving and almost naked, but the lieutenant got them through."

"What a hero he is," Jane said enthusiastically. She wondered if he and Susan might be engaged? In novels, men often did fall in love with the girls they rescued from distress. No, that was impossible. Lieutenant Palliser loved her and only her. She was sure of it. A beam of joy lit up her lovely face.

"Yes, indeed," Mr. May went on, "And no sooner had the lieutenant brought the Browns to safety than he went back to the army. He must surely be fighting somewhere hereabouts, but we don't know exactly where."

"Ali's grandfather, the *Nawab*, sided with us," Mrs. May said. "He sent the Malior army to help with the attack on Delhi. Most of the *Rajahs* and *Nawabs* in this part of India took the British side."

"Why was that?" Elizabeth asked her father. This wasn't the sort of question her mother could answer.

"They know we are going to win eventually," he said, "and little as some of them like the Company's *raj*, they prefer it to the unknown dangers of a peasant revolt."

"But Ali, sad to say, did not agree with his grandfather," Mrs. May continued. "His grandfather begged him to stay at home, and he did succeed for a while. Ali came here several times to ask for news of you. He's such a nice boy."

"What happened after that?" Catherine asked. She felt sure she would never see Ali again.

"He ran away to Delhi to join the rebels, and he hasn't been heard of since. His grandfather is angry at him, but heartbroken too. They say that he never leaves his room. Ali is all the family he has."

"Oh, the poor *Nawab*," Fanny cried. Unlike her sisters, she had never met him, but the thought that he might never be reconciled with Ali wrung her heart.

"After Ali disappeared," Mr. May said, "James Keats decided to join the English force besieging Delhi."

"But he doesn't believe in violence," Jane and Catherine said, almost simultaneously.

"No, he doesn't But he wanted to work with the doctors and help save lives. He's still there. The English force has lost more men from disease than from fighting, and many of the diseases are infectious. So James is by no means out of danger. But we do get news of him, and so far he is well."

"That's good," Jane said briefly. Catherine was very relieved, both at the news and at Jane's cool reception of it.

"But what is happening with the siege of Delhi? Do the mutineers still hold the city?" Elizabeth asked, once again looking at her father.

"Technically, our side was besieging Delhi, but really, the mutineers had us pinned down in our position on the ridge. The *sepoys* kept sallying out of the city and attacking us. For a long time things were pretty bad. But the rebels never managed to take the ridge, even though they had far more men than we did."

"Why not?"

"It was a question of experience," Mr. May said. "No *sepoy* is allowed to rise above the rank of *havildar* in the Company's forces. A *havildar* is like a sergeant. So none of the *sepoys* really know how to command a large army. Again and again, they raced up the ridge, attacking with desperate bravery. Again and again, we beat them back. They never really tried another tactic. Their bloated, putrifying corpses piled up beneath the ridge, and the stench was intolerable. The gasses of decay inside the bodies made them writhe as if they were still alive. Swarms of blowflies, fat from feeding on the corpses, literally darkened the sky. And after the monsoon started, it got much worse. The ridge became a mudhole. Snakes driven from their holes —"

Suddenly Mr. May broke off. Was he mad? How could he have let himself rant like this in front of his daughters? These horrors were completely unfit for the ears of four innocent maidens. But when he thought about his countrymen's sufferings, he seemed to lose control. He felt deeply ashamed.

"Well, I think that will give you the idea," he concluded lamely.

Fanny did indeed look a bit green.

"But what is the situation *now*?" Catherine asked. "Are the men still on the ridge? Are they still in danger?"

"The force on the ridge is no longer in danger. Things began to improve in early August. John Nicholson arrived with the Moveable Column. He has been a tower of strength. The men say that he never sleeps. An elephant train got through early this month. The big guns it brought began to pound the city, and then our commanders decided that it was time to act."

"And did they?" Elizabeth broke in.

"Yes. Our men attacked Delhi at dawn the day before yesterday. They breached the city walls with less trouble than they expected. But once inside, they met fierce resistance. They are fighting their way through the streets, hand to hand, even as we speak. I am sure they will retake the city, but it may be a while before they do."

"I thought you hated General Nicholson, Papa, and Devender told us that he's done all sorts of terrible things since the fighting started," Fanny said wonderingly. "Yet you actually sound pleased that he is leading the force at Delhi."

"Ah, little Fanny," her father said solemnly, "your kindness is truly feminine. But in this case you are being entirely too softhearted. You know I have always loved India. I still do, even though the peasants weren't as loyal to me as they should have been. But you must remember the terrible massacre at Cawnpore. After that, the harshest measures are justified."

"Oh, no! What massacre? We've heard nothing about Cawnpore. Tell us quickly!" the sisters cried out.

"I can hardly bear to tell you. A group of English people at Cawnpore surrendered when the local ruler promised to protect them. But he broke his promise and slaughtered a hundred and fifty defenseless women and children—brutally. He threw their bodies down a well. Since then, our soldiers have not wanted to treat any Indian as a human being, and I am more sympathetic with Nicholson than I once was."

"Well, I'm not," Catherine exclaimed. "Violence escalates. Revenge and counter revenge growing ever more horrible! Someone has to stop it! No wonder James refuses to fight!"

Mrs. May's attention had wandered. She was gazing sadly at Jane. It seemed to her that Jane had lost all her beauty. The flowerlike bloom on her pale pink skin was gone. Indeed, the pale skin itself was gone as well. Her face was almost... leathery. And very brown indeed. Muscles stood out on her upper arms, but elsewhere she was painfully thin. Fortunately she looked healthy enough, so perhaps with proper food and rest she would regain some of her beauty. But perhaps not.

Mrs. May sighed heavily. What an awful and totally unexpected development. If only she didn't have to deal with it. She reminded herself that even this terrible blow was not the worst thing that could have happened. She must thank God that Jane was still alive. As for the advantageous marriage with Lieutenant Palliser, well, there was no reason even to dream of that now. At least Elizabeth was still as pretty as ever. Catherine and Fanny weren't really changed either, but then they hadn't had much beauty to lose. Oh, why did it have to be Jane?

"Where has Komal gone?" Fanny asked suddenly.

"She's on the veranda talking to the *dhobi*," Mrs. May said, "You know they are old friends."

"Oh, Mama, I wish you wouldn't call him 'the *dhobi*,'" Elizabeth snapped. "He has a name, you know. It's Devender. And he's our friend as well as Komal's."

"All right, Devender then," her mother said in a conciliatory tone. "He *is* a nice fellow. When he brought Komal here from Arjunabad, he was kind enough to bring the laundry as well."

"What laundry?"

"The laundry you hid under when you fled from Shivapur, of course. It was quite clean when the *dho —*

when Devender returned it, so we have decent clothes for you to put on tomorrow. Those rags you're wearing are simply disgraceful. You must bathe and go straight to bed. You all look exhausted. Devender can stay with us tonight."

The sisters went outside to say good night to Komal and Devender. They found the two servants locked in an embrace. Hearing their footsteps, Komal jumped backwards, upsetting one of the cane chairs that dotted the veranda. She quickly straightened her *sari*, which had slipped off her shoulder.

"Excuse us, please," Fanny said politely, averting her eyes.

"What's going on?" Elizabeth said, less courteously, but more frankly.

Komal answered softly in Hindi. She did not want Mr. and Mrs. May to overhear.

"Devender and I have loved each other since we were children, but he is an untouchable and I am a *kshatriya*. We cannot marry in India, so we have been working and hoarding our wages. Now, finally, after all these years, we have saved enough to leave this land behind us. We shall sail to Mauritius as soon as the mutiny ends and it is safe to travel. There we can get married. We will have a new life." Her eyes shone.

"But Komal," Elizabeth said, "you're our *ayah*. You always tell us we're like daughters to you. How can you even think of leaving us?"

Komal smiled. "I do love you like daughters. I proved this when I risked my life to help you leave Shivapur. I will miss you. But in your family I will never be anything more than a servant. I want to seek my own happiness, and I can do this only with Devender. Perhaps we will even have our own children."

"Of course, you are right, Komal," Jane said. "Love is the most important thing. We will miss you too, but it was stupid of us to think that all you wanted from life was to be our servant. Why did we think that, I wonder? In any case, we will keep your secret."

"In novels about India," Catherine said, switching to English. "The English hero always has an utterly devoted Indian servant, who doesn't even want a wife or family of his own. Like Ram Das in that terrible *White Dove of Delhi*. This supposedly proves that Indians love working for white people if the white people just treat them kindly. Ugh."

As if to show that she was determined to have a life of her own, Komal kissed Devender warmly as she left the veranda. The sisters followed her into a room where four beds were neatly made up with clean sheets and mosquito netting.

"*Memsahib* May has been keeping this room ready, in hopes you would arrive safely," she said. "I will be leaving you, but you still have a mother."

CHAPTER TWENTY-THREE: IN MEERUT

"We're back in British India with a vengeance," Elizabeth moaned, as the sisters dressed the next morning. "Do I really need four layers of underwear? Well, it doesn't do even to think of that, I suppose."

"No, it doesn't. From now on we must wear as many petticoats as Mama thinks proper. And I'll have to keep mine clean," Catherine said.

"I've just had a comforting thought," Elizabeth said cheerfully. "Perhaps our copies of *Pilgrim's Progress* went up in flames when Shivapur burned! I don't *ever* want to see mine again. That book was *far* too preachy."

"Oh, Lizzie," Fanny said, "how can you say such a thing? I love *Pilgrim's Progress*. I often wished I had it when we were in Murarmau. And I wish I had it here. It might help me deal with missing Krishna. That's the burden I'm carrying now."

"We're *all* going to have to take up our burdens again, Lizzie," Catherine said mischievously. "Mama told me last night that she expects us to visit Susan Brown and her father today. They are staying with the Beagleholes, who also escaped. We are supposed to condole with them about Mrs. Brown's death."

"Oof," Elizabeth replied.

The sisters and their mother walked towards the large bungalow where the Beagleholes and the surviving Browns were now living. Its previous owners had been killed on the first day of the mutiny. An Indian servant in a spotless uniform ushered them into the sitting room, where another servant wearing only a soiled *dhoti* was listlessly pulling the cord of a huge *punkah*. Curtains of damp and fragrant *khus khus* grass covered the windows. The grass had been moistened to cool the breeze that blew in from the garden. Thanks to the *punkah* and these *khus khus tatties*, the temperature in the room was quite bearable.

The sisters kissed Susan and shook hands with her father and the Beagleholes. Susan stared at Jane with her eyes wide open. She was clearly pleased at what she saw. Mrs. May winced.

"We are so very, very sorry to hear of Mrs. Brown's death," Fanny said, sincerely, with tears in her eyes. "She was a truly good woman, and we know you will miss her terribly."

Before his daughter could answer, Reverend Brown spoke.

"God is not mocked," he said in solemn tones, "In His holy scriptures, the Lord tells us that 'there will be a multitude of slain, and a great number of corpses.' This is the retribution He has prepared for the natives who killed Mrs. Brown. God's word gives no support to misplaced tenderness for human life."

It seemed to Catherine that Reverend Brown's mind had lost its balance. Of course, you couldn't tell a man in that condition that Christianity was supposed to be a religion of forgiveness. But she wished you could.

Seeing Catherine's expression, Mr. Beaglehole intervened.

"There, there Brown. We have the fellows on the run now," he said in a soothing tone. "It is far likelier that there will be too much vengeance than that there will be too little."

Catherine shot him a grateful glance. It was good to hear the voice of sanity. She quickly introduced a new subject, Lieutenant Palliser's heroism.

"Yes," Susan said, her face glowing, "until the *gujars* stole his sword, Lieutenant Palliser, or Henry as I call him now, defended me against any number of perils. Why, Henry actually decapitated a tiger as it was leaping at my throat. I think he would have fought the tiger with his bare hands in order to protect me. Hen..."

Mrs. May winced again and rose to her feet. "We must be going now, Susan," she said coldly. "We shall leave you to dream of Lieutenant Palliser."

Everyone looked shocked.

"I mean, we shall leave you to reflect on the debt of gratitude you owe him," she amended.

As quickly as possible, Mrs. May swept out of the bungalow, followed by her embarrassed daughters. The dignity of her exit was somewhat diminished when her wide hoops stuck in the doorway. She had to jerk them free.

"Really, Mama," Jane said as they walked back to the *dak* bungalow, "You might just as well have said out loud that you are afraid Lieutenant Palliser — or Henry as Susan so charmingly calls him — will prefer Susan to me. How could you humiliate me like that? I can tell you think I look awful, but you might at least keep it to yourself."

"Jane, darling, I don't think you look awful at all," Mrs. May said quickly. Her tone was lacking in conviction.

Jane was silent. She reflected that Susan's nose was as red as ever, but the thought did not console her. After all, her own nose was now quite brown. She personally thought she looked wonderful with her tan, but Lieutenant Palliser — Henry — might well disagree.

The next three days passed quietly at the *dak* bungalow. News came by telegraph that the British had finally gotten the upper hand and were driving the rebels out of Delhi. But details of the street fighting had not yet reached Meerut.

The sisters took up their usual activities. Elizabeth painted, and Fanny ran errands for her mother. Jane fussed over her clothes, but didn't enjoy it much. She wanted to work in the garden, using her newly developed farming skills, but she was too agitated to begin. Her romantic prospects, or lack of them, weighed on her mind. She felt thoroughly unsettled, and she often thought about the man she had killed.

Catherine started writing again. Poetry, fiction, anything that would help her remember and understand the incredible experiences she'd been having.

She also brought her diary up to date:

"Sorry I've neglected you, Diary, but it's been utterly hectic. Now that I have an unlimited supply of notebooks, I can write as much as I like. I don't even need to abbreviate to save space.

Here's where we are. This afternoon, everyone was in the parlor. Papa joined us for tea. Craving *jalebis*, I had just made a big batch and was inhaling them even faster than Mahin used to do. My dress was speedily turning orange, and Papa was carrying on, as usual about his paperwork getting into arrears. Fanny offered help him with it. Gulping down the last *jalebi*, I told him how she had tried to save his papers the day Shivapur fell. Fanny was too modest, of course, to tell him herself.

Papa beamed at us and started making a speech:

'You have had rather a rough road to travel this year, my little pilgrims, especially the latter part of it. But you have got on bravely, and I think your moral burdens are in a fair way to tumble off very soon. I see many straws that show me which way the wind is blowing. You have all become far more womanly since I left you for the countryside last autmn.'

'What makes you think so?' Fanny said. The rest of us were utterly speechless. It had never occurred to any of us that we'd become more womanly, in Papa's sense of the term!

'Look at this,' Papa said, taking Jane's hand, 'I remember when this hand was white and smooth, and Jane's first care was to keep it so. Now it is roughened by housework, but my dear Jane, I value the womanly skill that keeps home happy more than white hands or fashionable accomplishments.'

We couldn't bear to tell Papa that Jane's hands got roughened by working as a peasant and not by doing feminine tasks in the kitchen. These days Jane says that she wants to have her own farm after she gets married. I think Lieutenant Palliser is more the farming type than James. Or at least I hope so.

Papa then paid *me* a compliment——or what he thinks of as a compliment: 'Catherine no longer bounces, but moves quietly and cooks treats for us all in a motherly way that quite delights me. I rather miss my ambitious girl; but if I get a tender-hearted, helpful woman in her place, I shall be quite satisfied.'

Yes, Diary, he really did say exactly that. I guess it's my own fault for making those *jalebis*! I should have realized that would give him the wrong idea. It's true that I've learned to cook Indian sweets, but that doesn't mean I've turned into a quiet homebody with no ambitions. In fact, I'm the only one of us girls who *hasn't* changed at all. I'm a writer, and I always will be, even if I do get married. And why shouldn't a girl bounce if she wants to? Actually, I bounce as much as ever. Papa just hasn't noticed.

Of course, Papa had nothing but praise for Fanny. You'll have to imagine what he said about her for yourself, Diary— it's too utterly sticky to repeat.

But the oddest interaction was the one he had with Lizzie.

He told her, "Lizzie, I can see that you have learned to think of other people more and of yourself less, and have decided to try and mould your character as carefully as you make your little paintings. I am glad of this, for though I should be proud of a pretty drawing made by you, I shall be infinitely prouder of a lovable daughter with a talent for making life beautiful for others.'

Lizzie was terribly annoyed, perhaps because there really *is* some truth in Papa's remarks.

'Yes, I think more about other people than I used to,' she snapped. 'I admit it. But it's not because I've become a selfless little woman any more than Catherine has. I do things for people who really *need* help—and that is just a matter of basic human decency. I learned that in Murarmau. And while we're discussing my development, Papa, let me tell you that I am *not* going to use **chiaroscuro** any longer.'

Papa looked completely puzzled. But I thought I saw the connection.

At this tense moment, we heard a sort of scratching at the door. Komal opened it, and in stumbled Ali, filthy and exhausted, but apparently in one piece. I reached his side in one huge bounce and threw my arms around him, earning disapproving glares from both parents. Ali sank onto the divan, looking utterly dazed. He couldn't speak. Komal returned from the kitchen with a glass of sweet **lassi**, which he swallowed at a gulp. But he clearly needed some time to recover, so we took him into our bedroom to lie down.

While he was resting, I wrote this entry. But now I need some time to recover too, Diary, because I have the most agonizing writer's cramp. So I will stop here."

CHAPTER TWENTY-FOUR: ALI'S RETURN

When Ali came back to the sitting room, the girls questioned him eagerly.

"Delhi has fallen to the English," Ali said. "I fought there for two months, in an army of ex-*sepoys* and *Mussulman jihadis*—which is what holy warriors are called. I'm not that kind of *Mussulman,* so as usual I felt that I didn't really belong. But at least no one called me a black Englishman. That's the curse my grandfather put on me, and—"

"You mustn't be hard on your grandfather," Fanny said softly, "He only wanted to keep you safe. He loves you so."

"Does he? Well, maybe he does. But he didn't manage to keep me safe. I ran away from Malior to prove that I am an Indian through and through. When I got to Delhi, though, things were already going from bad to worse. The *jihadis* and the *sepoys* feuded instead of agreeing on a strategy that might actually work. We were short of food, and the only water we had came from a few brackish wells. It was awful."

Catherine wanted to save Ali from having to describe the run up to the British attack on Delhi.

"We already know what happened next, Ali. Papa told us. But we don't know exactly how things went after the English got into Delhi."

Ali smiled a bit. "That was the only good part," he said. "We were prepared. We let the British army into city without really trying to stop them. It was a trick. We had built all kinds of defenses inside the city, and when they came over the walls, we counter-attacked."

"What happened then?"

"You won't believe this, Catherine, but I grabbed an axe from a dead *jihadi* and laid about me right and left. I hacked men to pieces. My clothes were covered with blood. I hardly knew what I was doing. After a few hours, we managed to stop their attack."

Catherine shuddered.

"Many British soldiers couldn't resist temptation after months of suffering on the ridge," Ali said. "They looted liquor shops in the parts of the city they controlled. They staggered about, hopelessly drunk. It looked as if we might actually drive them out of Delhi. We even wounded the terrible General Nicholson."

"Was he *hors de combat*?" Catherine couldn't resist asking.

"Definitely. But then frightening rumors rushed through the city. We heard that the English troops were going from house to house, killing all the women and children. I think that rumor was false. But we also heard that they were plundering the houses of friend and foe alike and killing every man of fighting age. And this was true, I'm afraid."

Fanny moaned.

"No one in Delhi had expected such a blood bath. Most people thought that if the English captured the city, they would just restore order. Even *Delhiwallahs* who had always sympathized with the English were horrified by the slaughter and looting. They wanted to fight back."

"What happened then?" Elizabeth said breathlessly.

"A crowd gathered outside the Red Fort, where Emperor Zafar lives. They swore that they would fight to the death if he would lead them. And for a while, it looked as if Zafar would agree. But then one of his counselors got hold of him. The man was in the pay of the English. He told Zafar that sharpshooters would certainly kill him if he rode out at the head of the people. Zafar lost his nerve. He went back to the palace with his tail between his legs, saying he had to attend evening prayer."

"What a shabby excuse!" Elizabeth cried. "Oh, how much better off the world would be if there were no religion. Imagine!"

"Lizzie!" Mrs. May said in a startled tone. "Just suppose someone were to hear you."

"Well, religious differences were part of the reason Delhi fell," Ali said. "If only the rebels could have been Indians first and Hindus or Mussulmen second! But Zafar's behavior didn't really have anything to do with religion. It was just plain cowardice. After he deserted them, the people of Delhi had no leader. By ones and twos, they scurried away, to seek safety where they might."

"What did you do, Ali?" Catherine asked.

"I saw that my grandfather had been right all along. God *is* on the side of the big battalions. A sea of despair washed over me. I knew that the English would control all Delhi in a matter of hours. If they caught me, they would kill me. And they might torture me before killing me. Or blow me from the mouth of a cannon. Since Meerut is closer to Delhi than Malior is, I decided to seek safety with you. In short, I scurried away like the rest."

Ali's tone was bitter.

"Don't blame yourself, Ali," Jane said. "You did what you could."

"You shall stay with us tonight, young man," Mr. May added, "but tomorrow, you must leave for Malior before dawn. We wouldn't want anyone to see you in Meerut. You will be safest if everyone believes that you were with your grandfather all along, because he is a friend of the English. You can ride my horse. Inder will ride with you on the pony and lead the horse back once you get home. I'd go with you myself, if I didn't have so much paperwork to get through."

"Ali," Catherine said suddenly. "I've been writing a poem about India. I want to show it to you even though it's not finished."

A gleam of pleasure crossed Ali's sad face.

How intelligent dear Catherine was, Fanny thought. Fanny herself had been unable to think of anything that might distract Ali from his grief. She was worthless in a crisis. In fact, she was worthless, period. A familiar feeling of depression swept over her. But she tried to combat it. She reminded herself that she knew how to make charcoal. That she had not broken down during the mutiny and that Elizabeth, for all her brash talk, actually *had*, and more than once at that. Then she felt better.

Sitting side by side on the divan, Catherine and Ali bent over the notebook she had brought back from Murarmau. He read the still unfinished poem.

"I like that part about the dusty soil, Catherine. It doesn't exactly sound like poetry, but it's powerful. This verse is good, too." He read aloud:

"After the firelight red on angry faces,
  After the silence in the burned-out houses,
  Those who were living are now dead,
  Truths that were living now are dying..."

Catherine looked very pleased.

"I'm glad you like it. Praise from another poet is utterly worth having. But I'm still mostly a fiction writer. Can I tell you about my new plan for a novel?"

But Ali was unable to suppress a yawn. His brilliant black eyes began to close. Catherine put her arm around him as his head sank onto her shoulder.

Mrs. May had been watching them. It made her uncomfortable to see Catherine touching an Indian so familiarly. But she mustn't be unkind.

"Ali is falling asleep," she said quickly. "He looks thoroughly done in. Komal has made up a bed for him in Papa's study. Inder will wake him very early tomorrow, so we must say good-bye to him now and go to bed ourselves. When things settle down a bit, he can visit us again."

Catherine undressed and lay down. Pulling the sheet over her head, she went to sleep immediately. But her sleep was troubled. She was back in Murarmau, fighting a horde of *sepoys*. Papa appeared and attacked one of them with an axe. The man fell. She looked down, and there was Ali lying at her feet, blood pouring from a jagged wound in his neck.

Catherine cried out and woke abruptly. She was trembling. Thank the lord, she told herself, it was only a dream. Ali is alive, and I'm safe in my own bed.

But she couldn't get back to sleep. She began to think about Papa's plan for sending Ali to Malior. She didn't like it at all. Suppose Ali and Inder *did* meet English soldiers on the way? Why was Papa so sure they wouldn't? And if they did, the soldiers were bound to be suspicious of a dirty, ragged Indian who was riding a saddle horse and was attended by a servant in uniform. They'd be sure to question Ali. And then the cat would be out of the bag — although that was not the right phrase for the tragedy that would certainly follow. Perhaps "the fat would be in the fire" was better? No, even that was not nearly strong enough!

Thinking hard, Catherine slipped out of bed and put on her riding habit. Fortunately, it had been in the laundry that Devender brought back from Arjunabad. She didn't know what time it was, but she sensed that dawn was not far off. She tiptoed through the curtained doorway of the bedroom. She had come up with her own escape plan.

Catherine groped her way toward her father's study. At the door, she met Inder, on his way to wake Ali. Catherine put a finger to her lips. She and Inder went silently into the room. Ali was sleeping on Papa's big leather sofa, still wearing the clothes in which he had fled from Delhi. His sword lay on the floor beside him. Catherine and Inder had to shake him several times before he opened his eyes.

"Ali, you must change clothes with Inder," she whispered urgently. "Then you and I will ride to Malior together. I'll take Papa's horse and you will take the little pony. If we meet English soldiers, I'll tell them I've gone out for an early morning ride and you're my groom. Since we'll be riding through British territory, they ought to believe me."

Ali staggered to his feet and picked up his sword.

"No, you'll have to leave your sword behind. If you take it, no one will believe you're a groom. Grooms are *not* armed!"

Ali looked sadly at the sword, but didn't argue. He could see that Catherine's plan was much safer than her father's. Inder's expressive face showed that he also understood what Catherine had in mind. Catherine turned her back modestly, while Ali and Inder exchanged clothes. Then they all went out to saddle the horse and pony.

"Inder," Catherine said as she mounted, "when Papa and Mama wake up, please explain to them what I've done. Tell them I'll be perfectly safe. Of course they won't believe you, but there's nothing we can do about that."

Hardly daring to breathe, Ali and Catherine rode through Meerut. The sound of the horses' hooves rang in their ears. Surely this racket was going to wake the whole station? To their surprise, it didn't.

They had no sooner left Meerut behind than it began to get light. Catherine looked toward the east. At first the sky simply turned gray. But gradually the fluffy clouds floating near the horizon began to glow. The east was suffused with a lovely pinkness, as the edge of the sun rose over the horizon. The level rays flooded the open landscape.

Catherine gasped with delight. "The dawn really *is* rosy-fingered," she exclaimed. "I should have known that an utterly great writer like Homer wouldn't just make something like that up. After all, great writers have to be observant."

The two friends trotted on in silence. They felt calmer now that they were well out of Meerut. A few miles ahead of them the road would split, with one fork going to Malior and the other to Arjunabad.

They had almost reached the fork when their luck failed them. Two English officers were riding towards them from the Arjunabad direction, at no great distance. A meeting was unavoidable.

"Remember that you're my groom," Catherine said quickly. "Don't speak unless you absolutely have to. No matter what those men say about the rebellion, don't lose your head and start arguing with them. They've probably never seen you before, so we should be all right if you don't do anything to make them suspicious."

Clamping a social smile on her face, Catherine waved at the approaching officers in their spiffy uniforms. Moments later, she recognized them. Oh lord. Was such an awful coincidence even possible? It was.

For there, large as life, were Captain Jones and Lieutenant Stapleton. The very men who'd been playing polo with Lieutenant Palliser on the day of the Mays' picnic, before the mutiny broke out. The very men who had called Ali a black bastard who shouldn't be allowed to eat with white women. Even Mama, with all her prejudices about Indians, had found them thoroughly offensive. And they had stared at Ali so intently that day. They would surely recognize him now. How could they possibly *not* remember him?

Ali had the same thought. He gripped the reins, white knuckled.

"Keep calm, Ali," Catherine murmured as the two men waved back at her. "When they recognize you, I'll pretend to be utterly embarrassed. I'll tell them we're having a love affair. I'll say that we ride out to meet one another secretly in the early morning, you from Malior and me from Meerut. Then I'll beg them to keep my secret."

"But, Catherine, they're sure to tell their friends about it afterwards, whatever they may promise at the moment. A love affair with an Indian! The rumors would ruin your reputation. You'd never manage to get married. And think how your poor mother would feel. No, we can't do this to her."

"Don't be a moron, you moron," Catherine hissed angrily. She spurred her horse, so that she was a few paces ahead of Ali when the officers met them.

Catherine greeted Jones and Stapleton warmly, even batting her eyelashes in imitation of Jane's manner with men. But they didn't seem to respond at all. It was utterly unfair, Catherine thought indignantly, that only the pretty girls were able to use such tricks. Was Ali really going to die because she wasn't good looking enough to distract these men?

Beneath his waxed mustache and smug, sleepy eyes, Captain Jones's little mouth spouted mechanical pleasantries.

"My dear Miss May, what a long time it's been. And how delightful to see you. I was so happy to hear that you and your sisters survived the mutiny. You must tell Stapleton and me all your adventures — some time, that is. Right now, though, we have urgent army business. We must ride on immediately."

Tipping their caps mechanically, the two men cantered away towards Meerut. Each of them looked at Ali's face in passing, but neither gave the slightest sign of recognition.

Catherine dropped the reins in surprise.

"My goodness, Ali. They didn't really *see* you at all. They just assumed you were a groom because you were dressed like one. And because you are riding a pony."

"Perhaps they didn't recognize me because all Indians look alike to them," Ali said. "I always found that so insulting, but maybe it has some advantages."

As they turned onto the Malior road, Catherine reflected that there were also advantages in being less attractive than her sister. If Jones and Stapleton had bumped into Jane, they'd certainly have stopped to chat. And given some extra time, they might well have remembered Ali.

Besides, who wanted to be admired by men like that? James Keats didn't find her unattractive. He thought she was "a striking girl." He had told Lizzie so, and Lizzie had told her. James had more brains in his little finger than Stapleton, Jones, and Queen Victoria put together.

"Ali, you're incredibly gallant," Catherine said with a laugh. "I can't believe you wanted to sacrifice your life to protect my reputation for purity. Fanny will be *very* impressed when she hears that!"

Ali laughed too.

When they reached the Palace of Malior, Ali dismounted and went inside to find his grandfather. Catherine turned her horse's head towards Meerut, and began her ride home, leading the pony. She hoped she could reach home before bedtime. Fortunately, there would be a full moon.

CHAPTER TWENTY-FIVE: LIEUTENANT PALLISER

The garrison in Meerut began to get regular reports from Delhi. General Nicholson died of his wound after hanging on long enough to hear that his men had captured the city. Emperor Zafar was under arrest. The English executed several of Zafar's sons without a trial. The massacres of ordinary people continued. Thousands of *Delhiwallahs* fled to the countryside, experiencing the same hardships the fleeing English had suffered when the mutiny first broke out. Delhi was a shambles. But a sort of dark peace eventually fell upon the city. The surviving rebels left to regroup and fight elsewhere.

The May girls and their mother were sitting in the parlor discussing these events, when Komal ushered Lieutenant Palliser through the curtained doorway.

Catherine cast her eyes toward her sister. Jane looked a bit flushed, but more composed than Catherine had expected. Lieutenant Palliser's eyes took the same direction. Jane was wearing a simple white muslin dress, which accentuated her tan. The lieutenant stared at her for several long moments.

Mrs. May tried to think of something suitable to say, perhaps about the weather or the condition of the roads. But her brain just wasn't functioning. All she could do was wait in silence for the words that would end her hopes of a good marriage for Jane. Fanny blinked back tears. Elizabeth looked angry.

"My word, Miss Jane," Lieutenant Palliser suddenly

exclaimed, "You are more beautiful than ever, if such a thing is possible. You look like a perfect... goddess. There's so much ... *more* of you than there used to be, somehow."

Everyone was surprised. Jane glowed with pleasure. James will be disappointed, Catherine thought, which is too bad. But then he's sure to turn to me for consolation. She smiled.

Fanny breathed a prayer of thanksgiving. She felt sure now that each of her sisters would get to marry the man she loved.

Lieutenant Palliser finally stopped goggling at Jane. He turned to Mrs. May and said in his most correct tone, "My dear Madame, may I request the favor of a private audience with your fair daughter Jane? The fact that I must return to my regiment in a few hours will, I hope, excuse my abruptness."

Mrs. May answered with the starchiest propriety she could muster, "Certainly, lieutenant. I am sure Jane can have no objection. Lizzie, Fanny, Catherine, come with me to the veranda at once. We simply must inspect the bougainvillea for aphids."

Left alone with Jane, Lieutenant Palliser burst into speech. A flood of words poured out.

"My dearest Jane, though your modesty may lead you to deny it, I am sure you have long seen my passion for you. When you disappeared from Shivapur, I suffered as only an English gentleman can suffer. I lived for one thing only: to kill the villains who took you from me. So I joined General Nicholson's force. I was happy only when I was blowing a captured rebel from the mouth of a cannon. Or perhaps when I was setting fire to a village. Then I heard that you were still alive. I worried that I might be disappointed in your appearance when we met again, but I decidedly was not. Yes... you are as lovely as ever. And *I* have a large private fortune. Will you reward my devotion by giving me your hand in marriage?"

Lieutenant Palliser's face wore a self-confident smile. Jane could see that he had no doubt of a favorable answer. He held out his hand, expecting that she would grasp it. But Jane was in a ferment. The lieutenant was as handsome as ever, but in other ways he seemed *very* different. Was this really the man she thought she loved? How could he have said that she would pretend not to know he was courting her? Did he think she was dishonest? If she still felt the melting passion for him that she had experienced when she heard the Simhas making love, she would tell him frankly.

But did she? A man who could boast of blowing people out of the mouths of cannon? Who was happy while torching the hut of some poor family like the Simhas? She had killed too, but oh, how she wished she hadn't had to. Better to work as a peasant all her days than marry a man who gloried in slaughter.

But he was waiting. She simply must answer him. She suppressed her agitation.

"Lieutenant Palliser," she said formally, "I must decline the honor of your proposal. Once, it is true, I thought I loved you. I will not deny it. But during the last months, I have changed and so, apparently, have you.

We could never be happy together. Please accept my answer as absolutely final."

The lieutenant was flabbergasted. He winced with humiliation, and then glared at Jane angrily. She could see that he too was struggling for calm.

"You are a handsome woman, Miss May," he said in frigid tones after a prolonged, embarrassing pause, "but it is by no means certain that you will ever receive another offer of marriage, much less a better one. You have no fortune, and this may well undo the effects of your physical allure, which, after all, is not *that* exceptional. However, as you have told me to accept your answer as final, and have done so, I might add, in a most unfeminine tone, do not be alarmed at the prospect that I will ask you again. There are others who appreciate my virtues, though you do not."

He bowed stiffly from the waist and immediately left the room.

Jane couldn't believe the speed with which it had all happened. A tear ran down her cheek as she thought of her lost hopes. She had once been so sure that she would find both happiness and riches as Lieutenant Palliser's wife. Her mother was going to be awfully disappointed. But she wasn't sorry for what she'd done. Lieutenant Palliser—Henry—could marry Susan Brown and her shiny red nose tomorrow for all she cared. And it seemed that this was exactly what he was going to do.

Jane had only a few seconds to think before Mrs. May literally sprinted into the room, followed by her other daughters. Making a wild demonstration with her hands in the direction of the veranda, she gasped out, "My dearest Jane, what on earth has happened? The lieutenant rushed past us with a face like a thundercloud. He mounted his horse and galloped off without saying a single word."

"He proposed to me, and I rejected him," Jane said flatly, though not without a touch of pride. "I told him that I no longer love him. He didn't take it very well, all things considered."

Mrs. May moaned.

"Oh, Jane, how could you? Such a good match. And then too, he actually didn't mind that you've lost your bloom. I doubt there will ever be another man who says you're beautiful in your present condition. And your Papa is as much in debt as ever. Sometimes I wish I'd never had a family. The worry is killing me."

Catherine leapt to her sister's defense. How could Mama be so cruel to Jane? Catherine had never liked Lieutenant Palliser, and she hadn't *really* wanted Jane to marry him. She just didn't want her to marry James Keats if it could possibly be avoided.

"As her mother, you should take Jane's side," she said angrily. "You make Jane sound like a damaged knickknack that no one wants to buy. Lieutenant Palliser is a conceited ass. He used to make the most utterly unfunny jokes at Ali's expense. He's not nearly good enough for Jane."

"Yes, indeed," Fanny said surprisingly. "Catherine is quite right."

Jane's face lit up. Mrs. May moaned again.

"No, no, of course Jane shouldn't marry a man she doesn't love. I know that. But it seemed as if she *did* love him. The whole thing was so very suitable. And then I thought that you, Catherine, could marry..."

Her voice trailed off as she realized what she was saying, but her daughters all knew exactly what she had in mind.

At this tense moment, Mr. May walked into the room. He had been at the Beagleholes' bungalow, consulting with Mr. Beaglehole on official business.

"I have exciting news," he told his daughters. "James is back in Malior. Now that our men have captured Delhi, his services are no longer needed. So when he heard that Ali was home, he went to join him."

"Perhaps they will visit us soon," Mrs. May said, looking uncertainly from Jane to Catherine.

Elizabeth laughed. "Well, since James has no idea if it's Jane or Catherine that he wants to marry, he will probably hang around Meerut for quite a while before he can decide. We mustn't expect anything as exciting as the lightning attack the lieutenant just made on Jane."

Mr. May looked surprised, but said nothing. He would discuss the matter with his wife later, in discreet privacy.

Meanwhile, Mrs. May recovered herself. She spoke in a tone of authority.

"Lizzie, your sisters' marriage prospects are not a joking matter. The less said about them the better. We certainly don't want people to call Jane a 'spin.' And what is a spin but a girl who goes from one man to the next?"

"Yes, Lizzie," Fanny said. "I know you wouldn't want to harm Jane or Catherine, but you need to remember that idle jests may do a lot of harm."

"Oh, let's just get back to living our lives in the ordinary way," Jane said. "There's been so much disruption. Papa and Mama, I have to tell you that tomorrow I am going to start working in the vegetable garden with the *mali*. I know Mama doesn't want me to get even more tanned than I already am, so I will wear long sleeves as well as my *solar topee*. I hope you'll accept this as a compromise, Mama. But even if you don't, I am *not* going to sit around in idleness any longer. I know how to grow crops, and I like doing it."

CHAPTER TWENTY-SIX: A WELCOME PAUSE

After their daughters had gone to bed, Mr. and Mrs. May sat down for a serious talk. Mrs. May told her husband how Jane had rejected Lieutenant Palliser's proposal. She had no idea why Jane's feelings toward him had changed.

"The upshot of it all," she complained, "is that Susan Brown will probably be married before Jane. It's lucky for me that Mrs. Brown didn't live to see this. How she would have triumphed! I feel sure that she would have attributed Susan's success to divine intervention."

"Mrs. May!" Mr. May exclaimed with some surprise. "Do you realize that you are speaking ill of the dead? Can you be capable of such unwomanly malice?"

"Oh, you hardly know what I am capable of when I'm really pushed," she said with unaccustomed spirit. "Of course, I'm sorry that Mrs. Brown is dead, and so on and so forth. But that doesn't change the fact that she was an intolerable woman. My only consolation is that Catherine is almost certain to marry James Keats. Of course, he's not nearly as good a match as Lieutenant Palliser, but Catherine loves him. And despite Lizzie's joking, I'm sure that Catherine is the one he wants to marry. What can a girl of Lizzie's age know about romance, compared to a mature woman like me?"

"I'd be happy if Catherine gave up all this nonsense about becoming a writer and got married. But, my dear Mrs. May, I must say that I find Lizzie to be a very bright girl. Difficult though she so often is, I wouldn't discount her opinions. When James visits here, we will have to see how he behaves."

"Humpf."

Several quiet days passed before the expected young men appeared. Elizabeth wrote a long letter to Mr. Ghosh and Pushpa. Papa's *chuprassi* was going to carry it to Murarmau. Catherine added a postscript, addressed to Mahendra, in which *jalebis* featured prominently. Fanny wished she could write to the Simhas, but of course they couldn't read, so she contented herself with sending them a loving message via the Ghoshes. Jane sent no messages. She was spending a lot of time outside, planting vegetables. Her mother wondered if she regretted rejecting Lieutenant Palliser.

September was over and the cool weather had returned, when James and Ali finally rode up to the *dak* bungalow. The sky arched blue and cloudless overhead, and a flock of small white parrots was roosting in the big tamarind tree in the yard. Northern India was looking its best.

The two young men dismounted and leaped up the steps to the veranda, where Mrs. May was sitting with her daughters. They could see that Ali had recovered his strength. He was carrying a small, wrapped package, which he had taken from his saddlebag. While the girls were greeting James, he handed it to Mrs. May. It seemed awfully heavy for its size.

"Open it," Ali said, smiling.

Inside the package was a glittering, jewel-encrusted

goblet.

"Surely it's not...?" Mrs. May asked hesitantly.

"Yes, it is. Solid gold, with real gemstones. It's my grandfather's way of thanking you all, but especially Catherine, for helping me get home. I told him about our meeting with Jones and Stapleton. And about how Catherine was ready to disgrace herself to save my life."

"Oh, but we couldn't possibly accept such a valuable gift," Mrs. May said primly.

"Nonsense, of course you can. My grandfather is a very rich man. This goblet means no more to him than a sixpence would to you. Or maybe a shilling. He would be very offended if you sent it back. So you must just take it and say no more about it."

"Must we?" Mrs. May asked, brightening up. "Well, I do hope you're right, because this goblet could pay all Mr. May's debts if we were able to sell it."

"Sell it by all means then," Ali answered.

"Goodness gracious, Ali," Catherine said, "is the *Nawab* really giving us a fortune? This is utterly like the ending of a novel. The only thing that's missing is the discovery that I am really the daughter of Countess Hoity-Toity, exchanged at birth by the wet nurse. Or something of that kind."

Everyone laughed.

"Ali has appeared like a *deus ex machina*," Catherine continued. "That's what they call the god who is lowered down from some sort of contraption at the end of a Greek play. I learned about it at school in England. The god comes in and solves everyone's problems, just the way this goblet is going to solve Papa's."

They all gazed at the goblet.

"It's so lovely, I wish we could keep it," Fanny said. "But of course, we must be practical."

"We'll be able to give one another Christmas presents this year," Jane said happily. "And we can buy other things as well. I wonder if there's anything we need?"

"Oh, I don't think we'll have any trouble spending what's left over after Papa pays his debts, no matter how much it is," Elizabeth said dryly. "It's quite easy to spend any amount of money. The trick with money is how to *not* spend it."

"I wonder if the appearance of the *deus ex machina* means that *our* story is coming to an end?" Catherine asked. "So much has happened in the last few months. Maybe we are about to finish one phase of our lives and enter another."

"That's very clever, Catherine, but you have to remember that life is not a novel," James said with a smile.

"Oh, isn't it?" she answered enigmatically.

Mrs. May asked James about the siege of Delhi. He described the foul living conditions and the desperate bravery of both sides in the conflict.

Catherine could see that James was telling them the truth about his experiences. Thank heaven, he wasn't mincing his words out of respect for their supposed feminine delicacy.

But Mrs. May was distressed by James's frankness. Amputations, dysentery, lice, maggots in festering wounds — it was hard to say which of his revelations was the most unsuitable. But she knew that her three older daughters would snap at her if she tried to silence him, so she held her peace. Her power over the girls was not what it had been, she reflected sadly.

"Although we say that 'the British' were fighting the rebels in Delhi," James said, "most of our troops on the ridge were actually Indians. And every time I cared for one of our Indian soldiers, I thought of Ali, fighting on the other side. Whenever the mutineers went back to Delhi after an unsuccessful attack, I would go among the dead they left behind, looking for Ali. I felt sure that one day I would stumble over his body. But God was kind to me and that day never came."

"Yes, God has been looking out for all of us," Fanny murmured. "His hand can be seen in so many things that have happened."

"What are you going to do next, James?" Catherine said sympathetically.

Ali broke in. "My grandfather wants me to go to university in England, and I have decided to obey him. I need to learn more about how the English think, so that I can turn their own ideas against them. That's the only way we'll ever get them out of India. James is going with me."

"Yes, and I am leaving India for good. What I have seen these last months disgusts me. I feel sure that the mutiny was caused by the Company's injustice and arrogance. The very thought of being an Englishman in India is intolerable to me now. We all serve the *raj*, directly or indirectly."

"I know what you mean," Catherine said. She had never seen James so worked up. "The *Nawab* wouldn't have wanted an English tutor for Ali if he hadn't believed that the English will control India for many years to come. So even though you were working for the *Nawab*, the Company's *raj* was the real reason why you were in India at all."

"You've hit the nail on the head, Catherine. As usual."

"Oh, James, what a cliché!"

"Sorry. I forgot that I have to watch my language around you," James said, smiling again.

"And what will you do when you return to England — to earn a living, I mean?"

"Well, I don't wish to sound conceited, but I believe that I will be appointed professor of Indian languages at Oxford. So I will be able to keep an eye on my mischievous boy here."

James gestured in Ali's direction, and it was Catherine's turn to smile.

Mrs. May was very pleased. James and Catherine seemed to be reestablishing their former friendship without the slightest difficulty. Mrs. May glanced at Elizabeth, somewhat triumphantly.

"But I have a confession to make," James said. His tone had become gloomy. "Although I do not believe in war,

I killed a man while I was on the ridge."

"Really?" Jane asked. "How did that happen?"

"Our men were charging down to stop the attacking rebels. I saw one of our soldiers fall, hit in the leg by a bullet. I ran to help him, picked up his rifle, and got him to his feet. Just then, the rebels reached us. A bayonet was coming straight towards me."

"What did you do?"

"I let go of the wounded soldier, and with his rifle, I... shot my attacker. Then I fled back back to our lines in a panic. I forgot all about the soldier I had gone to help, but fortunately he did survive. We picked him up later, after the fighting ended. But even though I may have saved his life, I am ashamed of what I did. I violated my own principles."

"I understand how you feel," Jane said eagerly. "I also killed a man. While we were in Murarmau. Like you, I did it in the heat of the moment, in self-defense. I tell myself that it wasn't really murder, but it still feels awful."

"*You* killed a man, Jane?" James repeated. "You of all people?"

"Yes, me of all people. Perhaps you don't know me as well as you think. But in any case, I've more or less put it behind me now. There isn't anything else to do, after all. You have to go on."

"Yes," James said thoughtfully, "you do have to go on. And I will, though I'll never stop feeling that I committed a sin. It's good to talk about it to someone who's gone through the same thing. Ali wasn't much help, because he feels no guilt about the killing he did."

Mrs. May saw Jane smile warmly at James. And James was gazing back at her with much the same mooncalf expression that Lieutenant Palliser had worn.

Mrs. May sighed. She seemed to have been sighing a lot lately.

CHAPTER TWENTY-SEVEN: ALI INTERVENES

October passed. Ali and James visited often. Catherine spent time talking to James, but she spent even more time with Ali.

Ali and Catherine played chess together. They passed their favorite books back and forth and had many a heated discussion—Jane Austen's wit versus Currer Bell's passion, whether Zauq or Ghalib was the better poet.

While Catherine and Ali were together, James often went looking for Jane. If she happened to be working in the garden, he would join her and help out. Mrs. May heard them talking about the oddest matters—crop rotation and the high rates of interest charged by the *bania*, for example. But who were the *bania*? She had no idea.

Mrs. May was thoroughly puzzled by both her daughters. Catherine was clearly as fond of James as ever. Yet she didn't seem to mind when he sought Jane's company. Mrs. May could see that he wasn't put off by Jane's tanned skin or even by the awful clothes she wore for gardening! He was still attracted to her. But occasionally a look of pain would pass over his face. Why was he suffering? Perhaps Lizzie was right. Maybe he really was having trouble making up his mind.

Towards the end of the month, Susan Brown paid them a call.

"Lieutenant Palliser—Henry—and I are engaged," she

announced dramatically.

Fanny didn't want Susan to learn that Lieutenant Palliser had proposed to Jane only a few weeks earlier. That would hurt the poor girl's feelings so terribly. And Fanny feared that dear Mama was miffed enough to let this information slip out.

"Are you indeed?" she said quickly, before her mother had a chance to speak. "What wonderful news! We all thought that his liking for you might ripen into something deeper after he rescued you."

"Oh, no," Susan said complacently, "that is not by any means what took place. On the contrary, Henry has loved me from the very first moment of seeing me, in Shivapur long before the mutiny. He told me that he never even looked at another girl after that. He says our marriage was decreed in heaven."

Mrs. May made a small choking sound.

"I do congratulate you," Jane said with a smile. She wasn't quite generous enough to pretend that the news upset her, though she knew it would please Susan if she did. "And when is the wedding to be?"

"As soon as this evil rebellion dies down a bit. Dear Henry is a very important officer in the Moveable Column now that General Nicholson has gone to his reward. Henry asked me if I would mind postponing the wedding until our men are closer to victory, and I told him, 'Slay on and spare not! Remember Cawnpore!'"

"You might have suggested that he return with his shield or on it. That's what Spartan women told their sons in ancient Greece," Catherine said dryly.

"Soldiers don't fight with shields nowadays, Catherine. Surely you know that? Henry is very sad that we can't marry immediately, but of course duty comes first."

"Oh, certainly," Fanny said gently.

Soon afterwards, Susan took her leave.

"Why don't I say it *for* you Jane?" Catherine asked. "Her nose is as red as ever."

The two sisters smiled at each other.

A few minutes later, Ali came in alone. Jane went out to the vegetable garden, and he asked Catherine to play chess. They sat down at a small table in the corner of the room. Watching them from the corner of her eye, Mrs. May saw that the game wasn't progressing very quickly. They seemed to be absorbed in conversation.

That night, Catherine wrote:

"Well, Diary, it's been a day of revelations. Susan engaged to the lieutenant! Jane utterly unconcerned! But that is the least of it. Ali arrived and said he wanted to talk to me privately. Why, I asked him? Because James had confided in him under seal of secrecy, and he had decided to betray James's confidence to me!

I knew I should stop him, but... I didn't. Partly, of course, I was just plain eager to hear what James had told him, whatever it was. Avid, in fact. But also I do trust Ali. He's a good person, and he's fond of James. I didn't think he'd tell me anything that would hurt James in the long run.

So it turns out that James has been unhappy for some time, ever since he realized that he's in love with Jane and not with me. He told Ali that he likes me a lot, but just as a friend. He used to think that he was attracted to Jane only because she's so pretty and that a marriage shouldn't be based entirely on physical attraction.

But since he got back from Delhi, he has come to see that Jane has a mind of her own. So now he is utterly in love with her in every way. Well, *he* didn't say utterly—*I'm* the one who used that word, as I'm sure *you* figured out for yourself, Diary—but that's utterly what he meant.

So, Diary, you will ask me why James is unhappy, such being the case?

Because he believes that *I* am in love with *him*! That is the confidence Ali decided to betray. James said that he felt he had paid me such marked attention before the mutiny that he is bound in honor to make me an offer of marriage. And he is sure that I will accept! But he loves Jane so much that he has been postponing it from day to day.

It is of course rather insulting that James should prefer Jane, tan and all, to me—even now that my frocks are not quite as messy as they used to be. But when I asked myself if I really minded losing James, it darted through me with the speed of an arrow that the answer is a resounding... no. Whatever I felt, or thought I felt, for him has melted away by degrees, without my even noticing. Perhaps I am incapable of real love? James says he likes me a lot, but only as a friend, and I can return the compliment.

Ali added, 'I would never have spilled the beans about this, Catherine, if I hadn't been sure that you no longer care for James in that way—if you ever did. But that being the case, I thought it might save everyone a lot of trouble if you allowed me to tell James so.'

'Spill the beans to him immediately,' I said with dignity, wondering whether it should be 'spill the beans *to* him' or 'spill the beans *on* him.' Neither one sounded quite right.

Will I ever get married? I don't know, and frankly, Diary, at this particular point I don't care. I'm only eighteen, after all. I want to finish writing "The Sorrowful Land" and start writing a novel. I want to be as famous as Currer Bell. I want a lot of things, but James Keats isn't one of them. Except as a friend, of course.

So Ali is going to tell James tactfully that he's free to propose to Jane. Whether she'll accept him or not remains to be seen. In a way, I wish she wouldn't. Like James, I have more respect for Jane now than I used to. She's no longer the girl whose greatest wish was for a *solar topee* trimmed with eel feathers, or whatever.

No, I don't really want to lose my sister when I've barely begun to know her. Especially not now, when Ali and James are also going away. But Jane must be the judge of her own happiness, and I must wait upon events. Such is the wisdom that my great age has given me!"

CHAPTER TWENTY-EIGHT: MRS. MAY SETTLES THE QUESTION

Mrs. May saw that Jane wasn't happy. It was clear now that James really did intend to propose to her and not to Catherine. But Jane had taken to avoiding him as much as she could without attracting attention. Perhaps she had decided against him and was trying to spare herself the unpleasantness of rejecting his proposal. Mrs. May hadn't rejected any proposals herself, but she doubted that it was a truly enjoyable activity.

Mrs. May hadn't changed her mind. She still did not want Jane to marry James Keats. For one thing, contrary to all expectations, Jane was actually recovering her beauty as her tan began to fade. Once again, Mrs. May thought that Jane rated a better husband than a penniless prospective professor. Perhaps Jane realized this herself and it was why she was avoiding James? No... Mrs. May hardly dared hope that any of her daughters would behave as sensibly as *that*.

Then, too, there was the problem of Catherine. Even though she had gained a bit of plumpness through a steady diet of *jalebis*, she would never be a beauty. A match between her and James was still very suitable. Catherine could hardly hope to be chosen by someone as eligible as Lieutenant Palliser, and she obviously liked James a lot. But even if Catherine didn't catch him on the rebound, yes, even if he escaped from the family altogether, James Keats wasn't going to get his hands on Jane.

Jane kept her own counsel.

Hoping that her sister would finally decide to stay in India, Catherine asked her no questions about her feeling for James. Fanny didn't either. Her delicate sense of honor would not permit her to force a confidence on such a private matter. Elizabeth also kept silent. But she watched Jane from the corner of her eye as she worked on an elaborate, Rajput-style painting of the Murarmau marketplace.

"Everyone seems to be waiting for something," Mr. May said one evening. "I can't think what it could be. After all, we are now out of debt, thanks to the *Nawab*'s magnificent gift, and I have cleared away all my arrears of paperwork. What else is there to be concerned about? My little women, you must settle down and be contented with the pursuits that make home happy. You have had a long course of excitement, and now it is time to make yourselves useful to others."

His daughters stared at him, but did not speak. Papa's paperwork obsession was really beyond belief. Could he have failed to notice that Jane's fate was hanging in the balance? Elizabeth rolled her eyes in her accustomed manner. Fanny began to sew with redoubled vigor.

Finally, after many vain efforts, James caught Jane alone. Wearing a plain *solar topee* and an old frock that reminded her mother of a pillowcase, Jane was hoeing eggplants in the vegetable garden. Hearing footsteps behind her, she whirled around, dropped her hoe, and tried to flee.

"Please, dearest," James cried, seizing her hands to

restrain her, "hear me out, even if you must reject me."

He looked very unhappy. After a moment's thought, Jane decided to remain. She couldn't avoid this forever, so better to get it over with. She withdrew her hands and stood quite still, looking intently at the ground.

"Jane, my darling, you must know how much I love you," James said tenderly. "And I will pay you the compliment of telling you exactly what I feel. I respect your intelligence too much to hide anything from you. Though it may sound conceited or even insulting, I was sure a few weeks ago that you returned my affection. You seemed so happy when I visited. We had such wonderful talks. Yes, you even gave me some lingering looks. But then you changed, and I have no idea why. My dearest earthly wish is to have you for my wife. Not just because you're beautiful, though I have to admit that that is part of it—but because you're you. Will you please tell me how things stand?"

For a moment Jane's eyes flashed joyfully. Then she set her lips in a firm line.

"I cannot marry you, James," she said after a pause. "And I cannot explain why. You must not question me, but simply accept my answer as final. If you respect me as much as you say, you should be willing to believe that I have a sound and serious reason."

Really, she thought, I'm getting quite good at this. 'Accept my answer as final' is an excellent phrase. Shall I tell James that 'I will be a sister to him'? No, considering Catherine's feeling for him, that would be coming too close to the truth.

"Well, dearest," James said sadly, "I will not question you now, since you ask me not to. But I cannot accept your answer as final. Until I see you married to another man, I can never give up hope."

Dropping Jane's hands, James left the garden and walked around the big tamarind tree toward the front of the bungalow, where his horse was tethered.

As soon as he was gone, Jane sank down and covered her face.

Mrs. May had been watching from the parlor window. She decided that the time had come to interfere. She went into the garden and tried to raise her daughter from the ground.

"Jane, Jane, I'm so very worried about you. For goodness sake, tell me what has happened."

Jane struggled to her feet and brushed the dirt off her dress.

"It's nothing, Mama," she said as calmly as she could. "James proposed to me, and I rejected him. Finally. It's just the Lieutenant Palliser story all over again. There's really nothing more to say."

"Heaven be praised," Mrs. May said instantly. She felt quite lightheaded with relief. "I'm glad you *finally* realized that James Keats isn't nearly good enough for you. Why with your beauty, you can surely marry —"

"Mama! How can you say such a thing?" Jane asked indignantly.

Mrs. May saw that she had gone too far. But it was too late to take back what she had said.

"It's ridiculous to say that James isn't 'good enough' for me," Jane continued, "because he is the best man I've ever known. I'm proud that he loves me. He thinks for himself, and he cares for me because *I* think for *my*self too. Not just because I'm pretty. He may not be as handsome as Lieutenant Palliser, but I prefer his face. You must remember that there was something in the lieutenant's eyes at times that I didn't quite like."

Mrs. May did not remember it, but she got the general idea.

"You love him, then?"

"Yes, of course I love him," Jane said, drawing herself up to her full height and removing her *solar topee*. Her hair gleamed in the sunlight.

"Then why did you reject him?" Mrs. May asked. "I'm sure you didn't do it out of consideration for *me*," she added, somewhat bitterly.

"No, indeed, Mama. You know that I'm fond of you. We all are, if it comes to that. But your ideas about marriage and mine have always been different, and they're even more different now than they used to be. No, I didn't reject James because he's not what you call a good match. I turned him down for only one reason — because Catherine loves him. Think how hurt she'd be if her sister married the man she loved. I can't bear to do that to her."

"That is very womanly and indeed noble of you, Jane," Mrs. May said. "You have such an exalted sense of duty."

Frankly, Mrs. May reflected, she didn't care *why* Jane

had rejected James Keats so long as she didn't change her mind. A better match would come along in time. After all, Jane was only seventeen. And James *might* turn to Catherine for consolation.

"Mama, I'd like to be left alone," Jane said. "I'll go on with my digging. Hard work should calm me down."

"Yes, dear," her mother answered meekly.

No sooner had Mrs. May disappeared through the door of the bungalow than James reappeared.

"Jane, forgive me, I have behaved unpardonably," he said. But he did not sound at all sorry, and his face was glowing with happiness. "I came back when I heard your mother come outside to speak to you. I thought she might be angry with you for turning down my proposal, and I wanted to defend you. I must confess that I've been hiding behind the tamarind tree, listening with all my ears. Is it really true that you love me? That you turned me down only for Catherine's sake?"

"Mr. Keats," Jane said stiffly, "it was indeed unpardonable of you to listen in on a private conversation. How could you be so dishonorable? You must forget everything you heard, especially what I said about Catherine. She would be so humiliated if she knew that you had learned her secret."

"Jane darling, I've already admitted I acted dishonorably. But is that really so important? Sometimes one has to bend the rules a little. Yes, I eavesdropped. I felt that I simply had to understand your heart. That meant more to me than life itself.

Surely God will forgive me—and you should too."

Jane couldn't help smiling. She saw his point. To cover one's ears under such circumstances would have required a positively inhuman degree of self-control. But she forced herself to frown once again. She picked up her hoe and whacked the eggplants without really seeing them.

"In any case," James continued, "it's a very good thing I listened. Because now that I know why you rejected my proposal, I have something important to say. Catherine doesn't love me."

He told Jane about Ali's conversation with Catherine.

"Oh, James, I can't believe it. Can it really be true? Catherine has seemed so happy lately. I felt sure it was because she expected you to propose."

"No, I'd say she's been happy because she's decided that she doesn't want to get married at all. That she can go on with her writing. She's no longer conflicted about what she wants. At least for now."

"Oh, James," Jane said again. She threw her arms around his neck and turned up her face to be kissed. Minutes passed. The brain fever bird sang its maddening song in the tamarind tree, but neither Jane nor James heard it.

"I must go to your father and ask for his consent," James said finally, resting his hands on Jane's shoulders.

"Yes, do. It'll be fine with Papa, I'm sure, though I guess you know now that Mama is not going to be pleased."

They walked into the bungalow hand in hand. James sought out Mr. May in his study. Jane went into the sitting room to tell the news to her mother and sisters.

"Dear Mama, I know this will come as a disappointment to you, but I have to tell you anyway. James and I are engaged, and I am the happiest creature alive. Others have perhaps said so before, but no one with such a good reason."

"Engaged?" Mrs. May repeated in tones of horror. "But you just rejected him. And so firmly. How could you?"

"Well, let's just say I discovered that my reasons for turning James down proved to be mistaken. We don't need to discuss it further."

"Mistaken?" Mrs. May echoed, looking pointedly at Catherine.

"Oh, Mama," Catherine said in an irritable tone, "I —"

"Yes, mistaken," Jane said quickly, anxious to spare Catherine's feelings. "I finally realized what I should have seen weeks ago. Catherine doesn't love James. And I do, so there's nothing to stop me from marrying him."

"Nothing at all," Catherine said. "Certainly not anything that concerns me. I'm happy with things as they are. So, Jane darling, I wish you every happiness."

The sisters gathered around Jane and kissed her warmly.

"You know, Jane," Elizabeth said, "even if Catherine *did* still want to marry James, that wouldn't have been a very good reason for you to refuse him, considering that you love him."

"Why wouldn't it?" Fanny said in a mystified tone.

"Because Catherine would have gotten over it, that's why. She's no weakling. It would have been the kind of stupid self-sacrifice that Papa is always preaching. The kind of sacrifice that really *isn't* for the good of all."

"Yes," Catherine agreed, "it *is* more the sort of thing people do in bad novels than the sort of thing that makes sense in real life. And suppose James had proposed to me from a sense of obligation? He'd have had to pretend that he loved me, when it wasn't true."

"Well, maybe you're right," Jane said uncertainly. "Of course, James really would have married you if you'd wanted him to. But if that had happened, the two of you might not have been very happy in the long run."

"Mr. Ghosh would never have approved," Elizabeth said, as if this settled the matter completely. "He would say that James owed it to Catherine to tell her the truth. And that Jane should have considered her *own* feelings, as well as Catherine's."

"Where will you live?" Fanny asked. "Will you go to England with James? Will you really be leaving us?"

"Yes, we will *all* miss you," Catherine said.

"And what about farming? I hope you're not going to give that up?" Elizabeth asked sharply.

"I hope not. Farming is my chosen work. I don't want to dwindle into a mere wife. But we haven't had time to make plans. James and I will have to do a lot of planning after Papa gives his consent."

CHAPTER TWENTY-NINE: IN SHIVAPUR

It was Christmas Eve of 1857, and the Mays were back in Shivapur. When the Company's forces retook the station, it turned out that their bungalow had not been torched, perhaps because it was at the far end of the civil lines.

So the Mays returned, only to find that the house *had* been looted. It was a complete mess. Furniture smashed to bits, dishes broken. The grass matting was gone from the floors. Mr. May thought that the rebels might have fed it to their horses.

Komal, who was getting ready to leave for Mauritius, organized a massive cleanup project. The girls pitched in and followed her orders like a well-disciplined army. Devender came to help.

Elizabeth sighed when all four copies of *Pilgrim's Progress* turned up, scuffed but otherwise undamaged. She handed one of them to Fanny, who received it with a cry of ecstacy.

Mrs. May ordered new furniture from Calcutta. The bungalow looked a lot fresher than it had the year before.

The May girls were sitting together on the veranda, enjoying the warm air.

"This Christmas will be quite different from last," Catherine said, "thanks mostly to the *Nawab*'s goblet. There are piles of presents hidden in every closet. I hope I'll be getting a copy of Anthony Trollope's latest novel, *Barchester Towers*. I've asked Mama for it, at any rate. It's a sequel to *The Warden*, the book I bought for myself a year ago."

"Your tastes haven't changed at all," Jane said, "But mine have. I want different things from the ones I was dreaming about last Christmas. I've actually thrown away that ridiculous *solar topee* with the pelican skin and feathers that I bought with my one and only pound last year. This year, I'm hoping that Papa will give me a book on soil drainage."

"It was wonderful of Papa to promise you enough money to rent and stock a farm near Oxford," Fanny said. "You'll be able to start farming at the same time that James begins working as a professor. Dear Papa has been very generous."

"Yes," Elizabeth said, "you're right about that, Fanny."

"Am I really?" Fanny asked in surprise. Elizabeth so rarely agreed with her.

"Indeed you are. Papa wouldn't admit it, of course, but he isn't trying to control us the way he used to. He's actually using the goblet money to help Jane become a farmer. A woman farmer! And he's stopped making those maddening remarks about how women can't paint or write. I think he's even bought me some very expensive brushes as a Christmas present. If only he wouldn't keep telling me to start using *chiaroscuro* again, he'd be a completely reformed character."

"I love the Rajput-style miniature you did of James and me in the garden of Malior palace," Jane said. "It'll remind me of India whenever I look at it."

"Thanks, Jane. I wonder if Mr. Ghosh and Pushpa like

the painting of their sitting room that I did from memory. Pushpa told me that *Diwali* is the Hindu equivalent of Christmas, so I sent it to them as a *Diwali* present. I miss them both so much. But now that the rebellion is gradually ending and things are getting back to normal, there's no way we're going to be seeing much of them, is there?"

"I'm afraid not," Jane said, "Except for aristocrats like Ali and servants like Komal, English people don't spend time with Indians. That was true before the mutiny, and I'm afraid it's only going to be truer now. All this slaughter is not likely to improve relations between the races, to put it mildly."

"Ali will be in England at university for years," Catherine said. "So we won't be seeing much of him either. But at least he'll return to us some day."

"Yes," Fanny agreed, "we will be separated from many of the people we like best. Mama would hardly let me go all the way to Murarmau to visit a peasant family like the Simhas. That's why I asked Papa to send them some of the goblet money. I want to make Krishna's life easier. Oh, I want it *so* much."

"It's a step forward that you've actually asked Papa for something," Elizabeth said, "even though you wanted it for Krishna and not for yourself. Next Christmas, I shall expect you to take another step in the same direction. You must choose something *for yourself*, and you must *order* Papa to give it to you!"

"You're laying a terrible burden on me, Lizzie, but I'll do my best to bear it as it pilgrim should," Fanny responded, in a comically exaggerated version of her usual self-denying tone. Pretending to pick up a heavy bundle and sling it over her shoulder, she staggered forward dramatically and dropped to the ground.

"Why Fanny, you just made a joke!" Catherine exclaimed in surprise. "Or at least, a sort of a joke. I don't think I ever heard you do that before!"

Fanny only laughed.

At this moment, Mrs. May came up the veranda steps, looking unusually cheerful. She was wearing a bonnet decorated with cherries and a new dress of violet bombazine with a bustle.

"Well, dearies," she said, carefully positioning the bustle under her ample bottom as she sank into a chair, "I have just paid my bridal visit to Susan Brown, or Mrs. Henry Palliser as I should now call her. That girl hasn't changed a bit. She's her mother all over again. She was *not* pleased when I told her that we were going to church only once tomorrow. She said that since our Savior has blasted the heathen and blessed our army, we should go to hear His word at all three services. Little does she know how much trouble I had convincing Lizzie to go at all."

"And was her nose —" Jane began.

"Oh, Jane, honestly," Elizabeth snapped, "of course it was. And what does it matter what color her nose is anyway? It almost sounds as if you're jealous of her for marrying Lieutenant Palliser."

"Children, children," Mrs. May said, "please stop squabbling. You haven't yet heard my news. Susan told me that a cavalry regiment fresh from England is going to be quartered in Shivapur. They are arriving next month. And several of the officers are single men in possession of *very* good fortunes. What a fine thing for you girls!"

And looking from Catherine to Elizabeth, she smiled.

GLOSSARY

ayah: nursemaid

bania: moneylender

chapatti: flatbread

chuprassi: messenger

dacoit: bandit

dal: lentil stew

dhobi: washerman

dhoti: short men's garment, worn in place of pants

dupatta: long, muti-purpose scarf

durzi: tailor

ghat: bathing steps at the side of a river

gujars: tribesmen

khansama: butler

kist: tax payment

kshatriya: warrior caste member

lassi: yoghurt based drink

Maharajah or Rajah: king

maidan: parade ground

mali: gardener

memsahib: lady

Mussulman: Muslim

Nawab: ruler of a Muslim princely state

palki-garry: horse drawn carriage

paneer: cheese

punkah: large, hand-operated fan

raj: government (literally "rule")

Rani: queen

sahib: gentleman/ 'sir'

sari: women's garment, worn in place of a dress

sati: custom whereby a widow burned herself on her husband's funeral pyre

sepoy: Indian soldier in the East India Company's army

solar topee: a hard hat thought to protect Europeans against the Indian sun

zamindar: landowner